Four Beautiful Letters:
BDSM

Desire Island Series – Book 4

Claire Thompson

Edited by Donna Fisk & Jae Ashley

Cover Art by Mayhem Cover Creations

Chapter 1

Nick Kincaid's heart kicked up a notch as he watched the Dom lower the bound, naked submissive into the water. His mind instantly veered to that delicious, dark fantasy realm where there were no limits—no safewords. She would be bound in rope and chain, utterly helpless. Her eyes would widen with fear and desire as the water closed over her head. He would keep her balanced on the precarious edge of trust and terror, his to control…

Nick blinked rapidly, forcing the dark fantasy from his mind.

Before submerging Skylar, Caelan Macauley, their seminar leader, had wrapped her ankles together using a strip of latex with Velcro at either end. He'd bound her wrists in front of her with another strip. "Rope is sexy, but you want something you can pull away quickly in the water," he'd explained.

Caelan stood in the plexiglass submersion tank, which was like a small, above-ground pool maybe four feet in depth, the top surrounded by a wooden platform set on sturdy beams. He cradled Skylar in one arm, his other hand over her nose and mouth.

"Her safe signal," he said, "is to raise her bound wrists above the water. That's what you will all use today."

Though quite a few seconds had passed, Skylar showed no signs of tension or agitation. The bound woman was utterly still beneath the water. Everything about her exuded acceptance.

After what seemed like an awfully long time, Caelan finally lifted his girl from the water. She drew in a deep breath, her eyes fixed on her Master.

"Thank you, Sir," she said softly, her face radiant with submissive adoration.

"My pleasure," Caelan replied, gently stroking the wet hair from her face. The love that moved between them was palpable. In spite of himself, Nick experienced an almost painful clutch of longing for what they seemed to share.

Caelan pulled the bindings from Skylar's wrists

and ankles and set her gently on her feet. As they climbed out of the tank and dried off, Caelan talked about the necessity of working closely with your sub to assess their skill with breath control and their comfort level with under-water bondage. "If you're new to this, start slow. And subs — don't hesitate to use your hand signal if you need to. Safety first."

Skylar climbed down the outer ladder of the tank, her hair streaming like wet honey down her back. She lowered herself to a padded mat nearby, the serene glow still on her face.

"Who wants to try it out first?" Caelan, who had remained on the platform, asked.

There were six attendees at the demonstration. Before Caelan had done the sexy demo, they'd each been asked to give a short introduction stating their name, their BDSM orientation and their experience level in the scene. Now the short, round man of about fifty who'd introduced himself as Marty got to his feet. He and his wife, Susan, didn't play at clubs, Marty had explained, but had been in a D/s relationship for over twenty-five years.

"We'll go," he said now, pulling Susan, who was equally short and round, upright. Both had on bathing suits, and Susan wore a gold choker with a padlock dangling from its front.

The woman who'd introduced herself as Sophia sat at the end of the row to his right. Nick guessed her to be in her late twenties or early thirties. She had blue-green eyes, in rather striking contrast to her dark hair, which was a riot of long, springy curls. While the couple on his left were both dressed in leather fetish wear, Sophia wore a brightly-patterned sundress, flip-flops on her feet.

Nick returned his focus to the tank. Marty and Susan had chosen not to use the binds for their first submersion experience, and Susan had opted to keep her bathing suit on. As he watched Caelan guide them, Nick's gaze drifted back to Caelan's sub, Skylar.

She sat back on her haunches, her hands resting on her thighs, a calm, serene expression on her face. She had introduced herself as a staff slave and as Master Caelan's personal property.

If someone was so willing to give herself over to that degree, would it be difficult as a Dom to avoid the slide from consensual submission to something darker?

"Who's next?" Caelan asked, once Marty and Susan had returned to their seats, wrapped in large towels.

Sophia rose from her seat. "I'd like to go next."

She glanced toward Nick. "Care to join me?"

Nick got to his feet. "Sure," he replied. "Let's do it." He had worn his swim trunks in place of shorts. Now he pulled off his polo shirt and kicked off his sandals.

He was pleasantly surprised when Sophia reached for the hem of her sundress and lifted it over her head. Underneath, she was completely naked. Her breasts were full and round, the nipples like pink cherries against tan, smooth skin. She had a triangle of neatly-trimmed pubic hair covering her cleft, which Nick found refreshing. Maybe he was showing his age, but he didn't particularly like the shaven little-girl look that was the fashion with most women he encountered.

Sophia was shorter and curvier than the slender, leggy blondes he usually went for. Yet, he found himself attracted to her just the same. There was something about her self-possessed confidence that was attractive, and also something of a challenge.

"Have you engaged in water play before?" Caelan asked Sophia as the three of them stood together on the tank platform.

"Not like this," Sophia replied. "Not in a submersion tank. But I'm quite comfortable giving up control."

"That's a good thing," Caelan said. "Especially if you choose to be bound."

"Oh, I *definitely* want to be bound," Sophia said, deep dimples appearing in either cheek as she grinned. "I love, love, love bondage."

"Then you're in the right place," Caelan replied, smiling back at her.

He turned to Nick. "What's your experience level with water play?"

"I don't have a whole lot of experience — just the occasional bathtub adventure," Nick replied. "Though I did engage in a submersion tank scene once at a BDSM club in Munich," he added.

That scene had ended almost before it began, but Nick didn't want to get into a lengthy explanation just then. It was over a decade ago now. He'd been twenty-eight and no novice to the scene, but he hadn't known his scene partner for more than a few hours.

Within fifteen seconds of submersion, she'd started thrashing and sputtering beneath the water. He'd immediately let her go, and she'd reared up, shouting in German that he'd tried to drown her. Hopefully, this scene wouldn't be a repeat of that debacle.

"If the two of you were on your own, you would need to bind Sophia while she was already in the water. But since there are two of us," Caelan said to Nick, "I'll bind her and hand her down to you. You can go ahead and get in."

Nick climbed into the tank. The water was warm and came up to his chest.

Caelan lifted Sophia with apparent ease. Nick, at six foot two, was plenty tall, but Caelan was taller and built like a linebacker. He held out his arms as Caelan crouched over the water and handed Sophia down. It was pleasing to hold a naked, bound woman against his chest. Her hair smelled good, like lemons and lavender.

Caelan sat down on the platform and dangled his legs into the water as he reminded Sophia of her hand signal and reiterated safety protocol with Nick. "Since this is just a demo and not an actual scene, it's a good chance for you to get a feel for your comfort level and breath control," he said, directing his attention to Sophia. "So I'm going to suggest you remain submerged for as long as you're comfortable, and then use your hand signal when you're ready to come up."

"Works for me," Sophia said.

Looking to Nick, Caelan added, "You, of course, will instantly lift her out of the water at that point."

"Got it," Nick agreed.

He placed his hand over Sophia's nose and mouth as Caelan had shown him. Then he lowered her until the water closed over her face. Blocking out everyone else around them, Nick kept his focus solely on Sophia. He half expected her to rear up after a few seconds like the girl in Munich, but she remained still, her body relaxed as she floated just beneath the surface.

Nick's cock tingled, his balls tightening with lust. Again his mind shifted to that dark place without limits or safewords. He held her floating body in one arm, his hand around her ribcage, the other protecting her nose and mouth in the water. He could feel the beat of her heart, a rapid tattoo. Was it excitement? Fear? Both?

As he held his breath along with her, Nick's heart began to pound, the pressure building in his face. Unable to help it, he opened his mouth and gulped in a lungful of air. How the hell was she staying under for so long?

He glanced up at Caelan, who was watching them intently. "Should I lift her out?" he queried.

Caelan held up a hand. "Not yet. It's been less than a minute. She's not at risk."

Nick looked down at the inert girl. While he was aware a person could safely hold their breath for two minutes or more, this felt like longer. But if the resident pro was okay with it…

Finally, she lifted her bound hands into the air, making the agreed upon signal.

Nick instantly lifted her above the water and removed his hand from her nose and mouth.

Sophia drew in a deep breath as she blinked rapidly. "Wow." She laughed, shaking her head like a puppy and splashing Nick in the process. "That was fucking *awesome*. I wish I could have managed it longer." Her eyes were sparkling, her body trembling.

Watching her excited reaction, Nick experienced a sudden rush of euphoria, as if he'd been submerged along with her. He grinned back at her, his cock tenting his shorts. Apparently, there was more to this girl than he'd first assumed.

~*~

Sophia entered the huge dungeon that evening, excitement fizzing in her veins. The place was filled with state-of-the-art BDSM equipment, each scene station equipped with its own set of impact toys and bondage gear. There were trained Doms and subs moving through the crowd, assisting with a scene here, spotting a difficult activity there, even offering their services in direct participation. The smell of leather, sweat and sex was ripe in the air.

Her first day on Desire Island so far had exceeded her expectations. In addition to being a first-class beach resort, the place definitely lived up to the glowing reviews and accolades it had received at various online BDSM sites she subscribed to.

The water play seminar that afternoon had been both informative and intense. While Sophia wasn't particularly looking to hook up with anyone during her week-long vacation, the guy she'd been paired with for the water play session was very easy on the eyes. She guessed he was somewhere between thirty-five and forty. He was maybe six foot two, his body lean and muscular. His hair was a rich, deep sable brown with glints of gold. He had a strong nose and jawline, his eyes dark, his lips full.

He had given off a sexy, dominant vibe that had added erotic tension to the scene. When he'd put his hand over her mouth and nose in the moment before guiding her under, something edgy and dangerous had sparked in his eyes. Just thinking of it now sent a shudder of desire through her body.

She tugged at the bottom of her black leather bustier, wishing it weren't quite so confining. She'd bought the ensemble—a leather bustier and matching leather skirt, along with ankle boots with more of a heel than she was used to—especially for this trip.

She adjusted the strap of her tote bag, which contained a bikini top and batiked sarong she might change into later, if the fetish-wear became uncomfortable.

When the seminar had ended earlier that afternoon, Nick had mentioned he was thinking of checking out the dungeon party, assuming he could finish some last-minute business he had to attend to. She'd said she, too, was planning to be there. Though neither had said it outright, Sophia hoped they would pick up that evening where they'd left off with the water play.

Someone tapped her shoulder. She turned expectantly, her heart constricting with a small jolt of excitement at seeing Nick again.

"Hello there, sexy lady," a man of about fifty with sandy-colored hair graying at his temples said. He wore a black leather vest, unzipped to reveal graying chest hair. There was a pair of metal handcuffs dangling from the belt loop of his too-tight leather pants. He had watery blue eyes and a nervous but determined smile. His gaze moved hungrily over her body, lingering at her breasts. Finally, looking up at her face, he said, "I'm Steven."

"Sophia," she replied, accepting his offered hand.

"You up for a scene?" he asked eagerly. "I'm wicked good with a cane and I'm looking for a naughty girl to use it on."

Sophia had had her fill of posturing Doms and wannabe Masters over her years in the scene. But Desire Island wasn't just some random club. One of the biggest draws for Sophia about the place was its exclusivity. The merely curious couldn't just book a reservation and show up with their whips and chains. Every potential guest had to go through an extensive vetting process to determine their experience level in the scene, and provide proof of a clean bill of health.

Steven wasn't exactly her type, but Sophia tried never to judge a book by its cover, especially in the scene. For all she knew, Steven might be an incredible Dom. And she did love a good, whippy caning. The skin on her ass prickled with anticipation.

She was just opening her mouth to agree when she spied Nick coming into the large room. His eyes met hers and he lifted his hand in greeting, a smile moving over his face.

"I'm sorry," Sophia said, turning back to Steven. "I'm here with someone tonight. But it was nice to meet you."

Steven pressed his lips together, a scowl flickering briefly over his face. Then he smiled and shrugged. "Okay. See you around."

As he melted away, Nick approached her. He looked good, dressed in a black knit shirt over dark jeans, black Gucci loafers on his feet. He had a gear bag over his right shoulder—a promising sign. As he got closer, she noticed the watch on his wrist, elegant in its gracious simplicity. Clearly, the guy had both money and taste.

"You got here in the *nick* of time," she said, grinning at her own pun. "I was just about to give up on you."

"I'm glad you didn't," he said. He shook his head, his smile rueful. "I never should have taken that last phone call from New York."

"New York?" Sophia replied. "You're from the city?"

"I am," he agreed. "You?"

"Brooklyn. I have a small antique shop there, but I go into Manhattan from time to time."

Nick laughed. "I've traveled all over the world, and wherever I go, I meet someone from New York. Half the time it's someone I know."

"Small world," she agreed.

"Want to grab a drink at the juice bar?" Nick suggested, gesturing toward the long bar set toward the back of the dungeon.

"Sure."

They found two free stools near the end of the bar. A guy in his twenties was behind the counter. Shirtless, he wore the black leather slave collar she'd seen on a number of employees at the resort. "Good evening," he said as they sat down. "What can I get you? We have fresh squeezed lemonade, sparkling water, still water and all kinds of soda."

"I'll have a lemonade," Sophia said.

"Sparkling water for me," Nick added.

He turned to Sophia as they waited for their drinks. "So, you own an antique store, huh? That sounds cool."

"It is pretty great. The store was my aunt's until she retired two years ago. She still owns the building, which is a good thing because no way could I afford the rising rents in my neighborhood. When I was a kid, I spent every day after school there. And on the weekends, I would tag along with my aunt to estate auctions and garage sales. That's still my favorite part of the job—discovering gems hidden among the junk. I'll never be rich, but I love what I do."

"That's what matters," Nick agreed as the bartender set down their drinks.

Sophia took a sip of the tart, not overly-sweet lemonade. "I love your watch, by the way," she added. "It's a gorgeous piece." On closer inspection, she recognized the vintage Patek Phillipe. It was in pristine condition, set in a rose gold case surrounding a silver dial, held in place around his wrist by a black alligator strap.

Nick looked down at his wrist. "I found this in a tiny watch shop in London. It was way more than I should have spent, but it just spoke to me, if that makes any sense."

"Perfect sense," Sophia replied, liking him even more. "That's how I buy most of my finds. But I have to ask—do you remember to wind it?"

Nick laughed. "About half the time." He shrugged, adding, "I guess I'm kind of old-fashioned in some ways. I own a vinyl turntable, and I actually carry a real pen and notepad with me when I'm working."

"Hey," Sophia said with a laugh. "You're talking to an antique hunter. I get it." She took another sip of her drink and asked, "So, what do you do that takes you all over the world, notepad in hand?"

"I'm in real estate development. I'm based in the city, but I sometimes get involved in international deals. I also own a couple of private BDSM clubs in Manhattan and LA. That's one reason I wanted to come to Desire Island. I'm always looking for new ideas."

"Impressive," Sophia said.

"But boring," Nick said with a wave of his hand. "We didn't come to this dungeon party to talk about our work, right?" He swiveled on his stool, raking his eyes over her body, his eyes glittering.

A shiver of desire moved over Sophia's skin, her nipples stiffening beneath his assessing gaze.

"You stayed under for quite a long time in the submersion tank," he remarked, breaking the spell. "I was holding my breath along with you."

"You were?" Sophia grinned. Her grin fell away

as she recalled the dark, enveloping feel of the water closing over her head as Nick lowered her into the water, and the raw, visceral thrill as he held her down.

Nick nodded. "I was impressed with your breath control. And how calm you seemed to be. I'd love to see how you handle other sorts of sensory deprivation." He placed his hand lightly over hers on the bar.

The atmosphere shifted again between them, like bits of colored glass in a kaleidoscope falling into a sparkling alignment of possibility.

"There's nothing sexier than a sub, tightly bound, gagged and blindfolded, completely at my mercy, with no idea of what's coming next." His voice, already deep, dropped a notch, his dark eyes boring into hers. "She doesn't know if it will be a brush of lips over her skin, a twist of her nipples, the snap of a whip, or the bite of a cane."

"Oh," Sophia breathed softly, her heart suddenly pounding.

"I'm not much for casual play, Sophia. If we scene together, every boundary you thought you had will be challenged. Every limit tested. Every sensation explored." His grip on her hand tightened, his eyes hooding as he gazed directly into her soul.

"Does that work for you?"

Chapter 2

Sophia drew in a sharp breath. This man — this virtual stranger — had somehow intuited her darkest fantasy. *Every boundary challenged... Every limit tested... Every sensation explored...*

"Oh, yeah," she said eagerly. "That works for me."

"Great," Nick said. "That station over there with the swivel sling just came free. Let's go grab it." He slid from his stool and hoisted his gear bag onto his shoulder.

"Yum," Sophia said eagerly, also getting to her feet. "I've seen those before. They're motorized, right?"

"Yep," Nick agreed, flashing a grin. "Round and round she goes, and where she stops, only her Dom knows."

"Cute," Sophia said with a grin. There was a

playful side to this man. Too many guys in the scene took themselves way too seriously.

They made it to the station before anyone else got there. The swing was beautiful, made out of a single piece of black leather with attached stirrups and a chain at each corner. The chains joined together in an apex that hooked onto the motorized carabiner.

Nick placed his hands on Sophia's shoulders. "I plan to secure you in the swing so you can't move. I will gag and blindfold you. You will be unable to stop the scene except with a safe signal." He studied her face, his expression serious. "Do I have your permission to take full control for the duration of the scene?"

She stared back at him, her heart doing a fluttery dance in her chest, her nipples pressing hard against her bustier. "Yes, Sir."

Sir? Where had that come from? Sophia never went in for protocol. But somehow the honorific had slipped off her tongue of its own accord.

"Good," he said, his eyes blazing with an inner fire that caused an answering heat to leap to life deep in her belly. "Strip out of those sexy clothes. I want you completely naked for this."

Sophia nodded. She took off her things and set them near Nick's gear bag. She watched with eager anticipation as he adjusted the height of the swing. He helped her up, settling her feet into the leather stirrups so that her legs were extended and spread wide.

She gripped the chains on either side of her as she watched him unzip his gear bag. He pulled out a purple silicone double penetration vibrator still in its original packaging, along with a tube of lubricant.

"Whoa," Sophia breathed. "That thing looks pretty intense."

Nick smiled. "It is. Do you have a problem with intense?"

"No," she replied staunchly. After all, this was why she'd come to Desire Island — for intensity of experience. "I can handle it."

"I'm sure you can," Nick said with a smile. He squirted lube over both heads of the toy. "Scoot forward on the seat. I want full access to your cunt and ass."

Sophia shifted her bottom on the smooth leather. She glanced around at the small crowd who had formed around the station. It was the same at the BDSM clubs she went to in the city. For every scene, you got an audience whether you wanted them there or not.

Crouching, Nick eased the lubricated double phalluses carefully into her cunt and ass. Aside from a flash of pain as the anal dildo fully penetrated, they went in easily. Nick clearly knew what he was doing.

Taking a step back, he said, "Since you're in a sitting position, you should be able to keep those in. Do they feel okay? Seated properly?"

"Yeah." The sensation of two silicone shafts inside her was actually quite pleasurable. This was going to be fun.

"Excellent," Nick said.

He cuffed and clipped her wrists to the back two chains of the sling. Returning to the gear bag, he pulled out a rubber horse-bit gag, also in its original wrapper.

Sophia's pulse picked up its pace. How had he known? She loved to be gagged, but hated ball gags. Bit gags were so much nicer.

As Nick buckled it around her head and fitted it into place, he said, "Remember, if you have to stop the action, use the club safe signal. You just open and close your hand in a fist. Okay?"

"Yrgg," she mumbled against the bit, showing him the signal with her right hand.

"Now the blindfold." He pulled a molded sleep mask from his bag of toys.

A shudder moved through Sophia's body as he placed it over her eyes. She felt deliciously vulnerable — cuffed, gagged and blindfolded — utterly at this man's mercy.

She gave an involuntary yelp of surprise when the dildos inside her suddenly vibrated to life. Pleasure coursed through her body, her clit throbbing from the vibrations radiating outward. Then the swing began to turn in a slow circle, adding to her sense of helpless disorientation.

Nick chuckled softly nearby. "That should be a nice distraction from the pain," he said. "You do understand there will be pain." It wasn't a question.

She jerked, reflexively tightening her grip on the chains at the sudden, painful flick of something against her inner thigh. *A single tail*, her brain informed her. It struck again, this time on her other thigh. Again she twitched, moaning against the bit.

The tail lashed her legs and snapped across her

shoulders, its strike random and biting as she slowly spun. Her nerve endings were firing in a confusion of pleasure from the vibrating sex toy entwined with erotic pain flicking over her skin at each snapping stroke of the whip.

Then, the heavy tresses of a flogger thudded over her shoulders while stinging leather flicked across the tops of her bare breasts.

How could Nick possibly deliver blows to both her front and back at once?

The answer dawned — he couldn't. Someone else had to have joined him.

The swing continued to turn. As she rotated, a whip cut across her nipples. She moaned against the gag, tears leaping to her eyes. The flogger crashed over her shoulders and upper back.

Around and around she spun as the cane, the single tail, the flogger and the vibrating sex toy continued their relentless assault. The sensations built, rising like a huge wave inside of her until she was mewling and trembling uncontrollably. The chains dug into her palms as she gripped them tightly. Her underarms prickled with perspiration, her breath labored against the gag, her heart thundering like a racehorse.

The dildos inside her ratcheted up in speed, the vibrations throbbing against her distended, aching clit. The pain and the pleasure rose in a wild, tumultuous crescendo of sensation. Her head fell back, her mouth opening in a scream around the bit as a powerful orgasm ripped through her body and exploded through her mind…

~*~

Nick and Dylan Gold, the staff Dom who'd assisted him during the scene, stood side-by-side, whip arms lowered, their eyes fixed on Sophia as she floated somewhere far beyond their reach. Her head was back, her lips softly parted. Her skin was flushed and faintly sheened with perspiration. A kind of inner light suffused her features as she drifted in post-orgasmic submissive subspace.

"She's something, your girl," Dylan said admiringly as they gazed at her. "She's still flying."

"She's not my girl," Nick said automatically. Realizing he sounded like an idiot, he amended, "That is, we only just met today. But, yeah. She's definitely somewhere up there in the sub ozone."

Gently, so as not to disturb her, he removed the dildos. Sophia sighed, but otherwise remained still, a soft, peaceful smile on her lips.

Her trusting surrender and powerful response during the scene had moved Nick in a way he hadn't expected. Normally a one-scene-and-done kind of guy, he was shocked to realize he wanted to take her back to his room to play with for the rest of the night. He pulled himself up short, however, not wanting to send the wrong signal or move too fast.

"Hey, there," he said softly as he removed the sleep mask from her face. "You okay?"

Sophia's eyelids fluttered open. She fixed her gaze on his face with a sexy, satisfied look. "Very okay. That was *awesome*."

"You took quite a whipping," Nick replied with a grin as he helped her from the swing. Power still coursed pleasantly through his veins. His cock was stiff in his jeans, but he was content to wait until later for relief.

Sophia swayed slightly as she got her bearings.

"I want to take care of those welts. Do you need to sit down?" Dylan asked, placing a solicitous hand on her shoulder.

"No, I'm good," she replied, standing taller. "Thanks."

Nick pulled the tube of specialty balm he kept

in his gear bag. As he stroked it into her skin, Dylan helpfully wiped down the swing and impact toys.

"Thanks for your help," Nick said to him.

"Yeah," Sophia added. "Thank you *very* much." She flashed a dimpled grin.

"My pleasure," Dylan replied with a smile. Turning to Nick, he added, "You've got yourself quite a little firecracker there." He lifted his chin toward Sophia for emphasis.

Nick laughed. "Don't I know it."

Dylan's eyes lit up as a woman with short auburn hair and large hazel eyes appeared. She wore a low-cut black minidress, her feet bare, a pretty red opal pendant around her neck that matched the one around Dylan's neck.

"There you are," Dylan said, kissing her on the nose. Putting his arm around her, Dylan turned to Nick and Sophia. "This is Kendra, my sweetheart," he said. "Kendra. Meet Nick and Sophia, two new guests to the island."

As they exchanged greetings, Nick was struck by the easy love that flowed between the pair, creating a kind of warm glow that surrounded them both. What would it be like to love someone like that, and to be so loved in return? Nick gave himself a mental shake. He wasn't even sure he knew what love was.

Grabbing their stuff, Nick and Sophia moved away from the scene station to allow the next players their turn. Nick pulled out the extra bottle of water he'd snagged at the juice bar and held it out for Sophia to sip.

She took a long drink and handed it back to him. "Thanks." Still naked, she held her clothes bunched under one arm.

"Can I help you back into that corset?" Nick asked, swinging his repacked gear bag over his shoulder.

"No, thanks," Sophia replied with a shake of her head. She opened her tote and pulled out a bright red bikini top and matching sarong. "I'd rather wear this, if you don't mind." She chuckled, adding, "Or even if you do."

He grinned. "I don't blame you. I have no idea how you women manage those tight-fitting outfits and stiletto heels."

"Oh, I draw the line at the heels, ," Sophia said, still smiling. "The corsets and bustiers make me feel sexy, and I love the scent of leather. But there's nothing sexy about a twisted ankle. Talk about torture devices," she added with a dimpled grin. "I never could learn to totter on those things."

Nick laughed. "You're funny."

"Uh oh," Sophia said, wrinkling her nose. "And here I was, going for sultry and mysterious."

Nick laughed again, in spite of himself. Who was this girl? He glanced around, wondering if he should take her to another scene station, or to one of the private fetish rooms for something more intimate. Maybe he'd just throw caution to the winds and take her right up to his room and…

"Hey, want to take a walk out on the beach?" Sophia asked, breaking into his thoughts. "I could use a little fresh air to clear my head. That scene was really powerful."

"Oh, uh, sure," Nick said, regrouping. She was right — there was no rush.

They left the dungeon and walked through the lobby to the main doors. Leaving their bags at the reception counter to collect later, they headed directly out to the beach.

The evening air was pleasant, a sea breeze stirring the air. They walked past the tiki bar, which was lit with hundreds of tiny lights strung around and between the palm trees. They passed small groups clustered around the fire pits, their faces lit by the flickering flames.

As they moved farther along the cool sand, the murmurs of the other guests were muted against the sound of the waves breaking along the shore. The sky was inky black overhead, sprinkled with tiny, sparkling stars.

"You handle yourself very well during fairly intense scenes," Nick commented. "I take it you have a lot of experience?"

Sophia shrugged. "I've been in the scene for years. I've gone to BDSM clubs and conventions and played with a lot of different guys, but nothing long term has really worked out. I did live with this guy for a while who identified as a Dom. I thought I loved him, and I definitely wanted to please him, but it didn't work out. He wanted me to try the whole Master/slave thing. I loved the BDSM play, and he knew what he was doing, so I figured, what the hell? I'd give it a shot." She laughed, shaking her head.

"Didn't work out so well, huh?" Nick surmised, trying to imagine this strong-willed young woman on her knees.

"You could say that," she agreed. "He did say

that," she added with a laugh. "I tried. I honestly did, but I couldn't get into the whole sub thing—at least not in the way he wanted. He wanted a docile, submissive slave girl who would massage his feet and say, 'Yes, Master,' to everything he said, even if it was bullshit." She chuckled. "He wanted to take full control of my life, down to what I spent on toothpaste and what brand of underwear I wore."

"How long did that last?"

"Two weeks."

Nick laughed. "That's thirteen days longer than I would have given it. You're definitely not the slave type."

"No," Sophia agreed with a rueful grin. "I've since learned to be more honest—both with my partner and myself."

"That's a good thing," Nick said. Though he normally gravitated toward just such docile, submissive slave girls, he found himself enchanted with this brash, self-confident, funny young woman.

"So," she said, turning to look at him as they walked. "Maybe you can explain it to me."

"Explain what to you?"

"What a Dom gets out of a BDSM scene. I'm not talking about the Master/slave dynamic. I'm just talking about the powerful interaction of pure, raw BDSM. I know what *I* get from it. The intensity, the erotic pain, the blinding pleasure, the excitement, the thrill of letting go, of total surrender. But you? You have to work so hard, and for what? Just to watch me go berserk?"

Nick laughed. "It doesn't feel like work to me. It's sheer pleasure. I love the look of erotic fear in a sub's eyes. I get off on the power of having complete control over her body and her experience. When a scene is good — when the connection is there — it's like I'm right there with you on that wild roller coaster of sensation and emotion. And to know I caused that — that I can give that to another person — it's amazing, really. But it's even more than that." He paused, trying to find the words.

"It's about trust," he said finally. "I guess if I'm honest, I don't trust very many people. I'm used to the cutthroat environment of high-stakes real estate development and backroom deal making. Some people in the business think nothing of pulling the rug out from under you if there's an extra nickel to be made. And when it comes to women" — he paused, not wanting to sound like a jerk — "well, let's just say there are some women who are more attracted to your wallet than to you as a person. Sometimes I find myself questioning their motives. I don't like to be like that, so I tend to keep myself to myself, probably more than I should."

"That's got to be rough, having all that money," Sophia said with a saucy grin.

"Oh, I didn't mean—"

"I'm just teasing," she said, her smile widening, her eyes dancing with good humor. "I get it. You want to be loved for you, not your Patek Phillipe."

"Something like that," Nick agreed with a grin.

He stopped walking, causing Sophia to stop too. He lifted her hand to his face and turned it so he could kiss her palm. He stopped himself in time. What was he doing? She would get the wrong idea.

Or was it the right idea?

He lowered her hand, but kept it loosely held in his as they resumed walking. "Back to what you asked—to what makes me tick as a Dom. Sometimes something happens. It's rare and I guess that makes it all the more special. The connection is just *there*. It's like an alchemical reaction—almost magical. There's no awkwardness. The trust is immediate and real. I felt it this afternoon in the tank with you, and I felt it again tonight."

He stared down into her eyes, which shone in the starlight. His lips tingled with the need to touch hers. He reached for her, closing his eyes in anticipation of her melting into his arms…

His eyes flew open as he stumbled forward into empty space, startled and confused. Sophia had pulled her hand from his and was running along the beach ahead of him, her crazy hair flying, the musical sound of her laughter floating back to him.

"What the hell?" he blurted, at first affronted and then amused. Laughing, he took off after her. She was fast, but he was faster. It didn't take long to catch up to her. He tackled her from behind, causing them both to fall to the sand.

Still laughing, he pulled her close. "Think you can escape me, huh?" he growled playfully.

She struggled, laughing too. "Let me go, you big bully. Let me—"

He cut off her words by covering her mouth with his. He held her close, enjoying the feel of her breasts pressed hard against his chest as he slipped his tongue past her soft lips.

She stopped struggling as she kissed him back, her hands coming up around his neck. They kissed for a long time, she cradled on his lap as he held her in his arms.

When he finally let her go, she rolled away and leaned back on her elbows, staring out at the water, which looked black against the blue-black, star-studded sky. "Wow," she said, turning her head to regard him. "You're some kisser."

"Yeah? So are you." Talk about understatement. He could have kissed her forever.

"It's a good sign," she continued, smiling at him. "If I don't like how a man kisses, I can't get past that. But you were perfect."

"I passed the test, huh?" he teased.

"With flying colors," she agreed easily. She sat up and swiveled so she was facing him. "So, what happens now? Where do we go from here?" Something sparked in her eyes. Longing? Desire?

"What do you want to happen?" he replied, not sure if he was going for playful or serious.

"I asked you first," she retorted with a grin.

He started to say something silly, but stopped himself. "Okay," he said slowly, gathering his thoughts. "I think it's pretty clear there's something happening between us. Like I said earlier today, I don't really go in for casual play. I admire your willingness and courage to give yourself over so completely. The way you let me submerge you in the water tank, and the way you reacted during the swing scene — it's clear to me that you crave intensity of experience."

"Yes," she said softly, all the playfulness gone now from her expression.

"We have this amazing facility at our disposal. We've barely scratched the surface in our brief time together, but it's enough to tell me I want more. A lot more. If you're interested, I'd love to explore your limits. I'm on the same page as you in terms of what I'm looking for. Or rather, what I'm not looking for. I have no interest in a Master/slave connection. But I would like to connect with someone who has the courage and desire to give herself over to me for the next few days. I want to go deeper than I've gone before. I want to take you with me on a journey of intense sensory deprivation, and see where it takes us both. I want to challenge us both. I want to go past fun into something real — something powerful. So, what do you say? You in?"

She didn't say anything for several long,

agonizing seconds. Nick held his breath, startled at how desperately he wanted her to say yes. He couldn't remember the last time he'd cared so much, or so quickly, about a woman. But Sophia wasn't like anyone he'd ever known before.

At last, her eyes sparkling, Sophia replied, "I'm in."

Chapter 3

Sophia woke early the next morning. After a delicious breakfast out by the pool, she took a swim in the ocean.

Nick and she had shared a nightcap at the tiki bar after their extended beach walk the night before. As they talked further, she had agreed that if things moved to a more sexual level as a result of the BDSM play, she was game to go all the way. Entrance to the island required a clean bill of sexual health, which took away that awkward bit of negotiation. When he'd asked about a condom, she demurred, explaining she was on the pill.

They'd arranged to reconnect that morning to begin a more serious exploration of sensory deprivation coupled with bondage and erotic torture. She hadn't seen Nick yet. He had probably been ensconced in his room making multi-million dollar deals. The thought made her smile. He was *so* not her typical kind of guy. She usually fell for the artistic types — the ones who didn't have two cents to their name. The ones who wrote poetry and played the guitar and had lots of dreams but rarely the ambition to bring them to fruition.

Nick was clearly driven, and that was okay. She was driven, too, even if what got her going was finding a gorgeous Blanaid crystal vase tucked away at the bottom of a box of Depression Era juice glasses she'd picked up for twenty dollars. Nick was obviously good at what he did, but he didn't seem to be overly-impressed with himself. She didn't get that sense of entitlement some Wall Street types seemed to wear like a second skin.

He was definitely dominant, but not obsessed with titles and protocol as so many players she encountered in the scene were. And he'd made her laugh, which was as important in Sophia's book as making her fly.

After her shower, Sophia selected a red tank top over a black sarong with a long slit up one thigh. She didn't bother with a bra. Even so, she almost felt overdressed on this BDSM island where half the subs went around naked or nearly so.

She arrived at the private bondage room on the second floor at the agreed upon hour of ten o'clock that morning. The door to the room was slightly ajar. Taking a deep breath, she tapped lightly and pushed it open.

Nick was already inside, his back to her. He turned as she entered, his face lighting in a wide smile that made her smile back. "Good morning," he said. "I was just getting a few things ready for our adventure."

He was shirtless, his chest smooth and broad. He wore black leather pants that accentuated his muscular legs and the rather attractive bulge at his crotch.

"Wow," she blurted. "You look good enough to eat."

"All in good time," he replied with a sexy grin. "Come in and close the door."

The windowless room was softly lit by sconces set along the upper walls. The space was dominated by a bondage table on one side, a St. Andrew's cross on the other. The back wall had a built-in counter with cabinets both above and beneath it. A recovery couch was set against a side wall next to a dorm-size refrigerator.

Along with a few items Sophia couldn't quite identify, Nick had set out various toys on the counter, including a vampire mitt, a sleep mask, several candles, an ice bucket and a set of rather sharp looking knives. Just the sight of the sexy toys got her nipples hard.

"Before we get started with the sensory deprivation, I think a good, hard spanking is in order."

"You do, huh?" Sophia said lightly, though her cunt instantly moistened with expectation.

"I do," he agreed with a smile, though his gaze left lines of fire over her skin. "Get naked and come lie across my lap."

Nick settled himself on the recovery couch as Sophia pulled off her clothing. Approaching him, she set her things on one of the arms of the sofa. She felt slightly awkward as she draped herself over his lap. The awkwardness fell away as he took hold of her wrists and extended her arms out against the couch cushions while simultaneously trapping her legs between his.

"Stick up your ass," he directed. "Offer it to me."

His hand came down hard, the slap echoing in the room as the sting spread in welcome heat over her skin. She adored being held down as his hand crashed down against her ass. She squirmed against his leather-covered thighs, the bulge at his crotch hard beneath her. He struck her again and again, each blow sending a jolt of perfect pain through her body and a flash of raw, throbbing desire through her sex.

When he finally stopped, she lay limp and panting on his lap, her cunt juices moistening her thighs, her heart hammering in her chest. A part of her wanted him to flip her over and rise above her on the couch. His pants would miraculously vanish so he could thrust his hard cock inside her.

But he clearly had other things in mind. He got to his feet, lifting her upright in the process. "Now that you're warmed up," he said in a low, sexy voice, "I want you to lie face-down on the bondage table. What's your safeword?"

"Mercy," Sophia gasped, still breathless from the intense spanking.

"Mercy," he repeated. "Got it. Since you'll be gagged for most of this session, your safe hand signal will be to open and close both fists."

"It takes a lot to send me over the edge."

Nick cocked one eyebrow. "Duly noted."

He helped her onto the table. Her entire body had heated up as a result of the spanking, and the leather felt cool and soothing against her skin.

There was a face cradle at the front of the table. She rested her forehead against the cushioned rim and closed her eyes.

Nick slipped leather cuffs around her wrists and clipped them to attachment bolts on either side of the table. He did the same with her ankles. Then he slid a pillow under her hips so her ass was raised, her cunt bared between her forcibly spread legs.

"I like you like that," Nick said from above her. "Naked, bound and on display. You can't move. You can't get away. You are indeed at my mercy, Sophia."

In spite of the fact that she trusted him, his words and the vulnerability of her position sent a tremor of delicious fear through her body.

"Do you have any issues with pump gags?"

A shot of adrenaline spurted through Sophia's veins. She lifted her head to see what he was holding. "I'm not entirely sure," she said honestly as she eyed the rubber contraption. It was similar to a ball gag, but instead of a silicone ball set into the leather strap, it had a small bulb-shaped head attached to a tube with a pump at its end. "I've seen them used, but I've never personally experienced one."

"This part goes in your mouth," Nick explained, holding the gag up for her to see. "Then I'll pump it until it's about the size of a small apple. Are you okay with that?"

Sophia swallowed hard as she stared at the ominous device. But this was what she had wanted, wasn't it? Intensity of experience with a Dom who knew what he was doing. If she was going to do this thing, she might as well go all in.

Wordlessly, she nodded.

"Excellent. Remember, if you start to freak out, just use your hand signal. Open and close both hands. There's no shame in that, no judgment. We're still exploring your limits right now."

His words calmed her. "Okay, yeah. I'm ready."

She allowed him to position the small rubber bulb between her teeth. He buckled the strap in place around her head and then used the pump to inflate the bulb until it filled her mouth. "Can you still swallow?" Nick asked. "I don't want to overinflate it. You need to be able to swallow."

Though her tongue was pressed back in her mouth, Sophia was able to swallow. The contraption was much nicer than a hard ball gag.

She nodded.

"Good. Now, try to make a sound."

Sophia managed a mewling squeak, but not much more.

Nick's smile was at once cruel and sensual. "Perfect," he purred, his eyes sparking with sadistic pleasure. He detached the pump tube from the mask and set it on the counter.

Turning back to her, he held up a padded sleep mask. "Next, we take away your sight." He slipped the mask over her eyes, plunging her into darkness. She resettled her head in the face cradle, her heart pumping hard.

"Now, your hearing."

Sophia felt the press of earplugs, which he adjusted until all she could hear was the whooshing beat of her own heart. She was truly helpless — gagged, bound, blinded and shrouded in silence. Her skin prickled with anticipation, all her nerve endings on high alert. She felt like a little kid on Christmas morning getting her first look at all the brightly wrapped packages under the tree. At the same time, it was as if she stood at the edge of a cliff, and the slightest push would send her flying…

A tickling whisper of something soft moved over her ass, startling her and causing her to jerk in her restraints. It fluttered down her thighs and flicked against her labia. It moved lightly over her back and brushed the sides of her breasts.

A feather?

A moment later, the sharp graze of dozens of tiny pinpricks moved over her skin. They scraped along her ass and the backs of her thighs just hard enough to get her full attention. Must be the vampire glove.

Then…nothing. For several long seconds she was left alone in the silence, her skin tingling, her cunt throbbing. She held herself rigid, tensing for whatever was coming next.

She startled at the sudden, thuddy crash of what could only be a flogger's tresses between her shoulders. The leather stung along her back and crashed against her already tender ass. She gurgled in pain against the gag, jerking in her restraints when the stinging tips of leather kissed her spread cunt.

The flogger was replaced by cool hands moving lightly over her skin. Nick cupped her flaming ass cheeks. She gasped against the inflated ball in her mouth as his fingers moved in a slow, sensual swirl over her cunt. She shuddered with pleasure as they slid inside of her.

All at once, his wonderful hands were withdrawn. She was alone again for several seconds in the silence and the dark.

She jumped at the sudden icy cold sensation moving over her ass and down between her legs. It took her brain a moment to catch up with her body and label the object as ice. He ran it along her labia and moved it in a frozen circle around her distended clit. Then he slipped the cube inside her, where it instantly began to melt in her heat.

She cried out against the gag when the icy chill against her skin was suddenly replaced with the sear of fire. Melted wax! It landed in scalding droplets over her skin, splashing on her ass and thighs. Then came the bite of a single tail where the wax had cooled, snapping it away in bursts of searing leather.

She didn't want to give up — to give in. She wanted to take whatever he meted out, but the sensations were piling atop one another, each new pleasure and pain adding to the wild, rising tide of feeling inside her. She was trembling, sweat slicking her body against the leather table, her heart racing as she struggled to breathe, nostrils flaring.

As the whip flicked, relentless against her skin, she tried to rein in her strong reaction. If she'd been able to move — to hear or speak or see — it would have been easier to handle. But held down as she was, the sensations were overwhelming. It was too much — she was going to have to use her safe signal. Panic washed over her like a bucket of icy water.

She jerked at her restraints, her hands about to make fists of their own accord when the restraints at her wrists were suddenly freed. The pillow was gently pulled from underneath her and her ankles, too, were released.

Strong arms lifted her, settling her on the table, this time on her back. But instead of removing the gag, blindfold and earplugs, Nick again restrained her, re-cuffing her wrists and ankles to the table so her arms and legs were spread wide.

Something cold and hard dragged along her throat and pricked lightly at the hollow where her clavicles met.

A knife!

What if he cut her, accidentally or on purpose? While she knew on some level that Nick would keep her safe, her body reacted on autopilot, the tremble rising from deep inside, her teeth actually chattering with fear.

One of the plugs was pulled from her ear. Nick's warm breath tickled her skin as he spoke, his lips brushing her earlobe. She relaxed at once, though her heart continued to race.

"Shh," he soothed, his hand cupping her cheek. "Calm down, Sophia. You're safe with me. I promise. All you have to do is remain very, very still. Give yourself over to the experience. Surrender to the blade. Surrender to me, Sophia."

As he spoke, he stroked her cheek and then moved his hand down her throat and onto her chest. He pressed his palm gently but firmly against her pounding heart. "I'll stop if you need me to. Just make the hand gesture."

His touch was soothing, his voice low and even.

She kept her hands still.

"Good girl," he said softly. "I'm proud of my brave girl. I know you want to feel the tip of the knife dragging along your skin. To know that with just a flick, I could draw blood. Eventually, we will go to that place, but not today. For now, I just want to play, Sophia. I just want to give you the promise of erotic pain—a taste of the freedom that comes from complete surrender…"

His words and soothing touch calmed her further, resettling her in a good place — a deeply submissive, receptive place. She wanted what he offered — all of it.

"That's it," he cooed. "You're mine, Sophia. Mine to control, to use, to torture, to adore…"

The plug was replaced, enveloping her once more in a vacuum of silence, save for the rush of blood pulsing in her ears. The blade slid again over her skin, its point drawing circles around first one nipple and then the other. It moved in a scraping line down her body. She stiffened, tensing as the cold metal made contact with her spread cunt. But it was only the flat of the blade that pressed between her legs. Still, just the proximity of that sharp knife moving over her most delicate parts made her tremble, her heart skittering and careening like a trapped animal against her rib cage.

Then the knife was replaced by something soft, wet and warm. It took her a moment to understand it was Nick's mouth against her sex. His tongue darted and licked. Already wildly aroused from the onslaught of sensation, she teetered on the edge of orgasm. Just when she was about to come, his perfect mouth fell away.

She was left alone in the silence for several agonizing seconds, her body thrumming with the thwarted need for release. Then she felt his weight as he joined her on the table, his warm, strong body over hers. The head of his cock nudged at her entrance. Her cunt spasmed, sucking him inside as she groaned against the inflated gag in her mouth.

The experience was like nothing she had known. She was unable to hear, to see, to speak or to move. Only her pelvis rose to meet his as he pummeled and swiveled inside her. His pubic bone was perfectly angled against her clit, and each thrust sent a deep shudder of raw, dark pleasure through her entire body.

Her brain short-circuited as he drew her toward a powerful climax. She was nothing but a cunt, her entire being fixated on that one part of her anatomy. His body was hot and hard against her, his cock filling her completely. Tears flowed from her covered eyes as she howled against the gag. When a hand circled her throat, the primal gesture sent her over the final precipice. She careened wildly into the most intense orgasm of her life…

The feeling of cool air on her face made Sophia open her eyes. The gag had been removed, as had the plugs and now the blindfold. She blinked as her eyes adjusted to the light. Nick stood beside her, smiling down at her. "You left the planet for a few minutes. You okay?"

She lifted her arms, reaching to pull him down into an embrace. "Yes. Oh, god, yes, Nick." She rained tiny kisses over his cheeks, his nose, his eyelids until they both were laughing.

Pulling gently away from her, he continued to grin down at her. "I guess that means you liked it, huh?"

She lifted a hand to wipe the happy tears from her eyes. "I fucking *loved* it. That was the most amazing experience of my life. Will you marry me?"

He took a step back, a look of alarm moving over his face.

She chuckled as she shifted to a sitting position. "Relax," she said, still chuckling. "That's just the endorphins talking. I have no designs on your freedom, trust me."

He smiled, shaking his head. "I'm sorry. Knee-jerk response. Of course I'll marry you."

"Wait, what?" Now it was Sophia's turn to be alarmed.

Nick's laugh was big and hearty. "Gotcha," he

said, pointing his index finger at her like a weapon. He bent down to retrieve his leather pants from the floor. He had a gorgeous body, muscular and tan. As he pulled the pants back on, he said, "Glad to know we're on the same page. Pleasure without strings. Intensity without obligation."

"Exactly," Sophia agreed, though a part of her wasn't quite sure what had just happened, or quite how she felt about it.

He helped her from the table and to a standing position. "Let me put some balm on your skin," he said, moving toward the counter. "Put your hands on your head and stand still."

Sophia obeyed. He smoothed ointment over her body and then led her to the couch. She perched gingerly on the cushions as he retrieved a bottle of water from the small refrigerator and handed it to her.

Nick glanced at his watch. "We only have the room for a few minutes more. How about we go get showered and changed and meet at the tiki bar in, say, thirty minutes? We can take a walk on the beach—maybe grab a bite of lunch if you want. Unless, of course," he added quickly, "you had other plans?"

"I'm signed up to attend a sensual yoga class

this afternoon, but that's not until three. I'd love to walk on the beach with you."

"Great. Then it's a plan."

She remained on the couch, sipping her water and basking in the afterglow as Nick wiped down the bondage table, cleaned his toys and put them away in his gear bag. They walked together from the room and down the hall to the elevator bank. She was on the third floor—he on the fourth. As she stepped out of the elevator on her floor, Nick stopped her, pulling her into a quick embrace. He kissed her mouth, his hands moving over her back. She melted against him as the doors closed again.

With a laugh, he let her go. "Sorry," he said, pushing the button to reopen the sliding doors. "I just had to kiss you. See you in a few."

"See you," she managed, trying to reel herself back down to earth, his kiss still burning on her lips. She floated down the hall to her room, unable to stop the goofy grin that spread over her face. This was turning out to be the best vacation ever, and it was only the second day.

Chapter 4

Nick whistled as he dressed for the evening. He'd gone snorkeling that afternoon with a small group led by Dylan, a man of many talents, apparently. While it had been a lot of fun, Nick was looking forward to seeing Sophia again. They had agreed to meet for dinner that night in the main dining room, and to go from there to the dungeon party.

He hadn't meant to restrict himself to just one woman while on this unique vacation, but somehow no one else he'd met held nearly the appeal Sophia did. He couldn't remember the last time he'd so enjoyed scening with someone. He sensed in Sophia a willingness to go as far as he was able to take her. The prospect was both exciting and a little unsettling. Who would be the first to draw the line?

He was just buttoning his shirt when his cell phone rang — the special ring reserved for his business partner, Brian. What the fuck? He'd told

Brian he wouldn't be available this week. Whatever it was, the guy would need to handle it on his own. He let the call go to voicemail.

He was just about to leave the room to head down to dinner when his cell, which he'd decided to leave behind, rang again with Brian's signature tone. It vibrated insistently on the desk beside his laptop as it rang, refusing to be ignored.

With a sigh, Nick went to the damn thing and looked at the screen. He saw there were several missed text messages and calls from earlier that afternoon when he'd been down on the beach. "Fuck," he muttered. "What now?" Without bothering to listen to the voicemails or read the texts, he punched the call back button.

"Oh, thank *god*," Brian said when the call connected. "Where the hell have you been? I've been trying to get you for hours."

"I've been on vacation, Brian. You know — that weird thing normal people who don't work eighty hours a week, fifty-two fucking weeks a year do. You should try it some time."

"Lucky for you I'm still on the job, Kincaid, because all hell is breaking loose with the Cabot apartment project. Two of the investors have pulled out because of some unanswered questions about the funding. Cabot is throwing a fit. I'm scrambling to get this handled, but you know the numbers side isn't my strong suit. I need you back here to take some of the heat off."

Nick blew out a breath as he sank down into a chair. Brian, younger than Nick by five years, was great at finding the deals, but not as good with bringing them to fruition. "Calm down," Nick said, trying to remain calm himself. He did *not* want to cut this vacation short. "I'm sure we can fix this. We've worked too hard and too long on this deal to let it fall apart now. I still have five days on the island, but then I'll be back and we can get this worked out. You just need to stall him for a little while, okay? Tell him I'm out of the country — whatever you need to do. Meanwhile, send me the details and I'll work on it later tonight, okay? A few days isn't going to make that much difference."

"I know it's your vacation, but we're talking a couple of million bucks here, if this pans out. Then you can take a lot more vacations."

"Chill, will you? Send me the stuff and I'll have a look. Meanwhile, call Cabot and see if you can't smooth his feathers a little. Tell him we're on the case and we'll get it sorted." Before Brian could protest further, he added, "I've got to go now. I have a dinner date."

Nick spied Sophia at a small table in the corner of the dining room, an untouched glass of red wine on the table in front of her. Her curly dark hair fell in ringlets around her face and over her shoulders. She was wearing a sexy low-cut black leather dress that hugged her breasts, emphasizing their cleavage. There was a small, secret smile on her face as she stared into the middle distance. Was she thinking of him?

He grinned at himself, shaking his head. He felt more like twenty than forty — a boy with a crush. It was both delightful and a little disconcerting. He reminded himself it was the intensity of the situation as much as anything. There were probably tons of budding romances on this BDSM resort island, where kinky sex drove most of the activities, and pheromones zipped and buzzed through the air like a swarm of bees. Folks no doubt connected all the time, passion flaring between them like a wildfire. Whatever might happen afterward, it made for a great vacation.

She saw him, her face breaking into a radiant smile, her dimples visible even from a distance.

"Hey, there," he said when he was close enough to speak. "Sorry I'm late. My business partner's having a minor meltdown."

Sophia quirked a brow. "Everything okay?"

"Yeah, yeah," Nick said easily, bending down to give her a quick kiss as he tried to ignore the anxiety in his gut. "It'll blow over, I'm sure." Except that he wasn't sure. The Cabot deal was huge, and they'd been working on it for months. If it fell apart now... *Stop it. This is more important than work.*

Whoa. Where the fuck had that come from? For Nick Kincaid, *nothing* was more important than work.

Still, this was the first time in a zillion years he'd taken any substantial time off, and damn it, he was going to enjoy it. He quashed his lingering anxiety. Brian would send him the details and he'd work on putting out fires later. Right now, he wanted to focus on the lovely woman sitting before him.

They passed the meal pleasantly, keeping the conversation light as they ate the delicious food. There was an early party at the dungeon, before the free play that would start at ten or so. The party involved BDSM parlor games, whatever those were, and Sophia had suggested they check it out.

They entered the dungeon together. There were already twenty or so people there. The young Brad Pitt lookalike who called himself Master Ryan was there, along with his red-headed slave girl. For a moment, Nick tried to imagine living a Master/slave lifestyle 24/7 on an island dedicated to the scene. No. He would miss his work too much. He would miss the constant excitement and opportunity of living in the greatest city in the world.

But for a week, it was fucking awesome to be there, and he planned to make the most of it.

Master Ryan called the guests into a circle. He stood in the center and explained, "Our first game is called Musical Doms. It's a great way to meet new people. All the Dominants please step forward."

Half of the group, most of them male but a few female, took a step forward, creating a smaller circle within the larger one.

"Good," Master Ryan said. "Now, turn so you're facing the sub standing behind you. When the music starts, the subs will walk in a circle. Doms, you stay where you are." He looked toward the outer circle. "When the music stops, whoever you're standing in front of is your Master for the next fifteen minutes. You'll engage in a quick scene of your temporary Master's choosing, and then we'll do it again. Any questions?"

Nick caught Sophia's eye. "This all right with you?" he asked softly. He would have rather just taken her up to his room, but if she wanted to play in the dungeon a while first, he would go along.

"Sure," Sophia replied with a toss of her head. "It's good to do a little comparison shopping."

"Ouch," he said with a laugh. "Hope I measure up."

The music started and the subs began to walk around the Doms. There were several very pretty women in the circle in various states of undress, but he found he wasn't especially interested. Maybe he'd get lucky, and Sophia would be the one to stop in front of him.

~*~

Sophia walked in the circle as the music played. This party was a good thing, she reminded herself. Nick and she had been moving awfully fast. There was an entire island of Doms to be explored. It would be crazy to limit herself to just one guy the whole time.

Especially a guy who was as driven in his career as Nick. From their casual conversations, she'd gotten the strong impression he lived and breathed real estate development. He was constantly putting together huge, complicated deals involving millions of dollars. He was still conducting business while on the island, for heaven's sake. A sole proprietor herself, she understood that your business didn't take a vacation just because you did. But she really didn't want to fall for a guy whose work consumed him. She'd been there and done that, and had promised herself she wouldn't do it again.

When the music stopped, she stood in front of a tall, heavyset man of around fifty dressed from head to toe in black leather, sweat gleaming on his broad brow. He grinned at her from beneath a thick mustache. "Hey, pretty lady. Looks like you're mine for the next fifteen." He moved toward her, circling her upper arm with his large, slightly damp hand. "You may call me Lord Larry. Let's go to the pillories. I'm going to spank that ass of yours until you squeal."

Oh, goodie, Sophia thought with an inward groan. Why had she thought this would be fun? Oh, well. She could handle anything for fifteen minutes.

She glanced toward Nick. His partner was a tall, willowy blonde in a black bustier with garters, a tiny thong barely covering her mons. She had small, high breasts and long legs capped by very high heels. Shit. She was fucking gorgeous. He was smiling at the woman, who was making a simpering face back at him.

Sophia turned resolutely to Lord Larry. "Let's

go."

They played the game two more times. Sophia didn't manage to get Nick either time. Happily, the guys she scened with, even Lord Larry, knew what they were doing. Her juices were flowing nicely from the spanking, flogging and hot wax treatment she'd received respectively from her three Musical Dom partners. She'd tried to ignore Nick and his scene partners, and she'd mostly succeeded.

As she headed back to the circle yet again, Nick waylaid her and murmured into her ear, "I've had enough. How about you? Want to blow this popsicle stand?"

"Sure," she agreed, glad he'd been the first one to suggest it.

As they left the dungeon, Sophia asked, "Want to take a walk on the beach? I hear there's a fire play demonstration tonight."

Nick put his arm around her. He looked very, very good in a black silk pirate's shirt open at the throat, soft black leather encasing his muscular legs. "I was thinking maybe we'd just go upstairs to my suite? Share a nightcap and…" He lifted his eyebrows suggestively, his lips quirking into a sexy smile.

"That works," she said, smiling back. She could see a fire demo any day.

When they stepped into his suite, they were greeted by a ringing cell phone.

"Shit," Nick muttered, striding across the room toward the phone, which quivered on the desk. "I probably better get that or he'll never leave us alone." He grabbed the phone, punched a button and held it to his ear. "What is it now, Brian?" He glanced back at Sophia, mouthing, "Sorry," before turning away.

She looked around his suite, which consisted of two rooms, unlike her single room on a lower floor. Moving toward the sliding glass doors that led out onto a balcony, she pulled them open. She stepped outside into the cool, moist air and leaned on the high railing to stare out at the dark ocean.

She'd left the door ajar, and she could hear Nick's deep voice rising with agitation as he spoke. He'd mentioned something at dinner about a possible snafu with a big deal he'd been putting together. "Okay, okay, Brian," he finally said. "Calm the fuck down. I'm opening the laptop now. I'll handle this, I promise."

Sophia turned back. Nick was seated at the desk now, booting up his laptop, the phone tucked between his shoulder and ear. She came back into the room and moved into his line of sight. "Everything okay?" she asked softly, a sinking feeling in her stomach.

"What?" He glanced distractedly at her and then seemed to focus. "Hold on a second, Brian. I said, hold on." He covered the phone with his other hand. "Look, I'm really, really sorry, Sophia, but I'm afraid I'm going to have to spend at least a little time on this. I feel like a total douche, but we've been working on this for months, and if I don't do a little damage control now — "

"It's okay," she said quickly, pushing down her irritation at the interruption to what was supposed to be a sexy night. "I get it. Life gets in the way, sometimes."

"Thanks," he said with obvious relief. "I really appreciate your understanding. Why don't you help yourself to something from the minibar while you wait? I'll just be a little while. I need to give this my full attention."

Sophia shook her head. She had no intention of sitting around watching Nick at work. She had a feeling whatever he was dealing with was going to take more than a few minutes. "You have my cell. Just shoot me a text when you're ready, and I'll come back up. The night's still young. I think I'll go check out the fire play demo on the beach."

Nick frowned and seemed like he was about to protest. But then he just nodded. "Okay. Thanks. I'll text you ASAP."

As he replaced the phone to his ear, she left his suite, closing the door with a click.

Sophia went outside onto the beach and approached the fire pit where the action was taking place. As she eased herself into the circle of spectators, she recognized the woman wielding the fiery whip. It was Ella Bertrand, one of the co-owners of the island, whom she'd met when she'd first arrived. In her late forties, Mistress Ella was beautiful, with silver hair and dark, almond-shaped eyes. She was wearing a caramel-colored vest and matching leather pants.

The Kevlar whip snaked in a fiery line through the dark. The person on the receiving end of the flaming whip was a tall, slender man in his twenties with a shaved head and a studded slave collar around his neck. He was naked, save for a codpiece covering his cock and balls. His arms were raised, hands behind his head, his back to the Mistress. Each time the whip met its target, he gave a small cry but held his position.

Sophia watched, fascinated, her skin tingling with desire to feel the flicking heat of the flaming leather against her own body. She wished Nick was there with her so he, too, could enjoy the energy and power provided by the scene. She slipped her hand into the pocket on the side of her dress and pulled out her phone. No text yet.

Whatever, she told herself. She returned her focus to the scene. Maybe Mistress Ella would take volunteers after the demo, and Sophia would raise her hand.

When the scene ended, Mistress Ella did, indeed, ask for volunteers. Several hands shot eagerly in the air, but Sophia's was not among them. What if Nick texted during the scene and she missed it? Even as the thought kept her from raising her hand, she mentally chided herself.

He was the one who had cut the evening short, or at least bisected it with his need to conduct his business. Why should she let his issues affect her fun? She raised her hand, but the selection had already been made. She watched as another girl shed her clothing and took her place as Mistress Ella prepared a new whip.

Sophia watched a while longer, but then drifted away, her heart no longer in it. She went to the tiki bar and ordered a frozen piña colada. While she was sipping, a nice-looking guy with light brown hair and light blue eyes slipped onto the stool beside her. He wore a tight black tank top, a black leather collar with an O-ring at the throat around his neck. He ordered a beer and then swiveled toward her. "Hi, there," he said in a drawling Southern accent. He had an overbite but it was kind of cute, and his eyes were kind. "I'm Kenny. I just arrived this afternoon. I'm a sub boy. Would you like to be my Mistress?"

She grinned and shook her head. "Sorry, Kenny. I'm in your camp."

His face fell, but then he shrugged with good humor. "Figures. You're lucky, you know. It's much harder to find a Mistress than a Master, even on Desire Island."

They talked amiably for a while about the scene in general and their own experiences in particular. "Maybe you can talk to the staff," Sophia suggested. "I bet there are dominant women here who would love the chance to get their hands on you."

Kenny looked hopeful. "You think so?"

"Sure," Sophia agreed. "You're a good-looking guy."

His face split in a broad, open grin. "Why, shucks, ma'am," he said with an exaggerated drawl. "Thank you kindly."

As they sipped their drinks and talked, Sophia's hand kept slipping of its own accord into her pocket. But her phone remained silent and still.

After a while, an older woman, maybe fifty or so, dressed in a too-tight black latex minidress and thigh-high boots slid onto the stool on Kenny's other side. Leaning across him, she addressed Sophia. "This boy toy belong to you?"

"No, ma'am," Sophia replied, infected by Kenny's southern accent. "I do believe he's available."

"Yes, ma'am," Kenny agreed eagerly, swiveling toward his potential Mistress.

She looped her finger in the O-ring on his collar and pulled him closer. "Get on your knees, boy, and tell me why I should consider you."

When she let go of the collar, Kenny slipped at once from the stool and knelt up, hands behind his back, eager as a puppy dog.

With a rueful grin, Sophia gulped the rest of her drink, set down her glass and rose from the stool. "Have fun," she said to the pair, who now only had eyes for each other.

She thought about returning to the dungeon for a little action. But the drink had gone to her head and she was tired. Back inside the resort, she selected a homemade cookie from the plate on the reservation counter and went up to her room. Once inside, she lay on her bed, still fully clothed, and munched on the delicious butterscotch oatmeal cookie. She pulled the phone from her pocket and set it on the nightstand.

If and when Nick texted, he could come down to her. She would get up in a minute to get changed and wash up. But first, she would just close her eyes for a little while...

Chapter 5

Nick awoke with a start. He lifted his head, groaning aloud at the painful crick in his neck. He was still seated at the desk in his hotel suite, the laptop open beside a pad of paper covered in his messy scrawl. It was dark outside. Where was his phone?

He glanced over the desk and lifted the pad of paper as he massaged his sore neck. No phone. Pushing back the chair, he finally spotted it under the desk. He leaned down to retrieve it. A glance at the screen showed him the time: 2:35 AM.

"Fuck," he swore softly. "Sophia."

He tapped the phone's screen to wake it up. There were no missed calls or text messages. Should he text her? Was it too late?

Maybe she was still up. Maybe she was down at a party on the beach. Or maybe she'd hooked up with someone else…

He blew out a breath, shaking his head at the thought. He had no claims on Sophia. They'd only known each other for a couple of days. But what a couple of days! He couldn't remember ever connecting with someone so quickly or so completely as he had with Sophia.

If only work hadn't gotten in the way.

Which reminded him...

He pulled the laptop closer and tapped a key to see if anyone had responded. While crunching a new set of numbers to try and salvage the Cabot deal, he'd also called and emailed various potential investors who might be willing to come in at the last minute to cover the shortfall left by the skittish bankers who'd baled on them.

"Yes," he cried triumphantly, seeing the email reply with the subject line: *Count me in!* Maybe he could save this deal yet.

He opened the email, read it and began to type...

The next time he opened his eyes, he was in the bed, or rather, on top of it, still fully clothed. The sun was streaming in through the glass, the sky a sparkling blue. He sat up abruptly, pushing his hair from his eyes.

His phone was beside the bed. He grabbed it and tapped the screen. It was 10:22 in the morning — over twelve hours since he'd said he'd text Sophia ASAP. What an ass he was. He'd let work get in the way of his vacation, damn it.

At least he'd saved the Cabot deal. Or rather, he'd gotten enough ducks in a row, if they all swam fast enough, to keep it afloat for the time being.

Thumbs poised, he quickly shot off a text.

"Good morning, Sophia! I'm so, so sorry I didn't text last night. I got insanely involved in trying to salvage this deal, and then I must have conked out. I just this second woke up. You still around? Can you forgive me? Want to meet for late breakfast? Early lunch? Skip food and head straight to the dungeon? Xxxooo"

He hit send and then stared at the screen nearly a full minute, willing her to reply.

The screen remained blank, the text unread.

"Fuck," he breathed, hoisting himself off the bed.

He shucked his clothing as he headed toward the bathroom. He turned on the shower and then used the toilet and brushed his teeth. Before climbing into the stall, he checked his cell once more.

Blank as a slate. Silent as a tomb.

He stood under the hot spray for a while, letting it pummel his head and shoulders. Then he soaped up, rinsed and climbed out. As he dried himself, he reached for the phone. No missed texts or calls.

While he was shaving, the phone dinged. Dropping the razor, face still half-covered in shaving cream, he grabbed it and tapped the screen. A text from Sophia!

"Yes, I forgive you. :-) Sorry, can't meet until this evening. Not knowing if/when I'd hear from you, I made other plans... See you at dinner around seven?"

Whew — she forgave him, and had even included a smiley face. But other plans? That sounded ominous. Did those other plans involve other guys? Not that he should be surprised — or even upset. After all, he was the one who'd dropped the ball. He could use the time to make a few more calls and to walk Brian through some things he needed for him to handle.

He typed back, *"Dinner sounds great. And what about after? You up for some sensory deprivation play?"*

This time her response was immediate. *"Always! What did you have in mind?"*

"I have something diabolically delicious in mind…" he texted, grinning. *"You want to hear it now, or should I surprise you?"*

"Oooh… I love surprises," she texted back.

"Excellent. See you at seven."

Sophia looked both sexy and adorable in a low-cut red top over a long, flowing skirt, her unruly curls framing a face kissed by the sun. She was hard to pin down, style-wise, sometimes appearing in fetish-wear, other times, like tonight, in hippy-chic. It was another thing Nick liked about her — she was her own woman.

He rose from the table as she approached him, relieved to see she was smiling. When he held out his arms, she stepped into them. He pulled her close, enjoying the feel of her soft, unfettered breasts against his chest.

They sat as a wait person appeared to take Sophia's drink order. Once he had left them, Nick asked lightly, "So, what have you been doing all day?"

"I went surfing," she replied.

Nick raised his brows. "Really? I had no idea

you knew how to surf."

"I don't. But Dylan and this really nice lifeguard named Josh were offering lessons for beginners." She grinned. "Not that I progressed much past hanging onto the board while they towed me around, but it was fun. I also attended a branding demo."

Her eyes widened as she placed a hand on Nick's arm. "Oh, my god, Nick. Mistress Ella — she's one of the owners — have you met her?" Without giving Nick a chance to reply, Sophia rushed on, "She branded her slave girl, Maya, right in front of us!"

Nick instantly visualized Sophia naked and bent at the waist over a tall stool. How she would tremble as the red-hot poker moved closer and closer to her flesh. How she would scream as the fiery metal seared deep into her skin. While his brain instantly rejected even the possibility, his perverse cock tingled, his balls tightening at the thought of delivering such extreme erotic pain. But aloud, all he said was, "That sounds intense."

"Yeah, it totally was," Sophia agreed, unaware of his dark imaginings. "First, she just talked for a while about safety and consent issues, and then she did a demo on a potato and let us all try it. It's harder than it looks. And then, she showed us the iron poker with the brand design Maya had commissioned from this BDSM branding site—a heart with Mistress Ella's initials inside it. You have to heat it up with a propane torch to exactly the right temperature—too hot and you can injure muscle tissue or cause too much scarification—too little heat, and the brand won't set properly. One of the guys watching passed out when Mistress Ella did the actual branding."

"Whoa. How did Maya handle it?" Nick asked, back in control of his dark fantasies. He remembered the petite blonde who had checked them in upon arrival.

"Like a champ," Sophia said. "She didn't make a sound. It's like she was in another dimension or something—some kind of submissive meditative thing—it was awesome to watch. It's not her first brand, either. She and Mistress Ella have been together for over ten years, apparently, and they're legally married and everything. They're both way into heavy erotic pain—Mistress Ella on the giving end, of course," Sophia added with a grin.

"You're pretty good at taking erotic pain," Nick offered, his cock hardening at the thought of flicking a single tail over her curvaceous ass. "Are you thinking of getting a brand?"

Sophia hugged herself, a shudder moving

through her frame as she shook her head. "No way," she said emphatically. "I'll stick to marks that fade after a day or two, thanks."

"Brands are definitely permanent," Nick agreed. "Even more so than a tattoo—you can't get a brand lasered off. You're stuck with it."

"Yep. It's for life. I can't imagine that level of commitment."

"Agreed," Nick replied staunchly.

He'd spent most of his adult life avoiding commitment. He'd dated plenty, and there were lots of available women, both in and out of the scene. Yet, even with women who'd lasted longer than a few months, he'd always kept his metaphorical bags packed, one eye on the door. He told himself it wasn't fair to expect some woman to sit around at home waiting for him all the time. His work always came first. At least until he'd made his first million.

Yet, he'd made that, and quite a bit more besides, but nothing had changed. He was too driven—his focus on finding the opportunities others had missed, gathering the resources necessary to make it happen, and achieving his goals.

Now he was forty—perhaps midway through

his life—and what did he have to show for it, other than more money than he knew what to do with? Thinking about Mistress Ella and Maya, and the incredible level of commitment they must share, his heart did a strange sort of twist. Imagine loving someone so much you would want to claim them in such a permanent way. What would it be like to give your heart so completely to another?

He was saved from further introspection by the arrival of their meal. Dinners in the formal dining room were family-style, the menu selected by the chef. Along with a delicious green salad and fresh bread, that night they were offered Cornish game hen stuffed with mushrooms and wild rice, or a vegetarian lasagna. Nick had chosen the hen, Sophia the lasagna.

Over homemade lemon-ginger ice cream, Nick said, "So, you ready to hear about the surprise?"

Sophia grinned, her dimples making small crescent moons in her cheeks. "About time. I was starting to think you were going to make me pull it out of you. I had an internal bet going with myself on how long I would last without demanding to know."

"So, who won the bet?" Nick asked, cocking an eyebrow and trying not to laugh.

She paused a moment and then, still grinning, asserted, "*I* did, naturally. But since you brought it up, now you have to tell me. Tell me, tell me, tell me," she added with comic eagerness.

Nick grinned back, anticipating the fun ahead. "I was able to reserve the vacuum bed chamber from eight thirty to nine thirty this evening." He fixed her with an intent gaze. "You ever tried a vacuum bed?"

Color rose in Sophia's cheeks — a good sign. "I haven't personally tried one. I've seen them before, though. Definitely not for the claustrophobic."

"Which you're not?" Nick asked hopefully.

Sophia shook her head. "Crammed elevators and crowded subways don't bother me. But then, I've never lain between two sheets of latex before and had all the air sucked out of them, so..."

"Well, tonight's your lucky night," Nick said with a grin.

He placed his hand over hers and leaned closer, lowering his voice as he stared into her blue-green eyes. "Just imagine, Sophia. Because the latex covers your face, you'll have to keep your eyes closed. As the air is sucked out, the bed closes down around you, completely immobilizing you. But because the latex is thin and molded to your body, it creates an effect like the skin of a drum. Each caress, every flick of a whip will be magnified by the vibrations across your skin, heightening sensation."

"Gosh," Sophia breathed, staring back at him. "How do I breathe?"

"There's a hole cut in the latex for your mouth. You stick your lips through it before I start the suction process. You'll be able to make sound and draw in air. But you'll have a safe signal, too, in case it's too hard to speak."

Sophia pushed her empty ice cream bowl away and eased her chair back from the table. She flashed an impish grin. "It's eight twenty-five. What're we waiting for?"

~*~

The sign on the doorknob was turned to the *vacant* side. As Nick opened the door, he flicked the sign over to read *occupied*. Once in the room, he turned on the light.

He looked hot, as always, dressed tonight in black jeans and a simple black T-shirt of thick, soft cotton that strained across his broad shoulders and hugged his nicely rounded biceps. She'd been mildly pissed at him for blowing her off the night before, but she'd decided to take a philosophical approach. The guy was clearly a workaholic but, happily, that wasn't her problem.

Now, Sophia took in the space. There was a counter at the back with various items set out on it, along with a sink and a small refrigerator. There was a recovery couch set against one wall. But the main attraction was a simple rectangular frame made from PVC pipes set out on a raised platform. A black latex sheet was already stretched taut inside of it, a second, clear sheet resting loosely on top of it. There was a round fitting secured to the bottom pipe, the vacuum hose already attached. The platform stood only about a foot off the ground. A small vacuum pump sat on the floor beside the platform.

Nick headed toward the counter, where he set down his gear bag. Turning back to her, he said, "We'll do a brief trial run with the vacuum pump, just to make sure you're okay with this. The sensation can be pretty intense."

"Have you tried it?" Sophia asked, curious.

"Not this particular one, but I've been in a vacuum bed," Nick replied. "I think it's important to experience everything I plan to do to my subs. Unless you've personally felt the cut of a cane, the stroke of a flogger or, yes, the intense sensation of a vacuum bed, how can you expect someone else to submit to it?"

Sophia tried not to snag on his use of the plural *subs*. After all, it wasn't like she wanted an exclusive relationship with the guy.

As she removed her clothing, she thought more about what he'd just said. "It makes sense, the way you put it. Most Doms, at least the ones I've met, have no idea what it's like to be on the receiving end of a whip."

"Then they're idiots," Nick said with a shrug. "Without that knowledge, how can you possibly give your sub the experience they long for?"

Sophia nodded, liking him even more. So many dominant guys in the scene were just about the power and the sexual thrill of taking control. Most of them were people she wouldn't have had anything to do with if they hadn't had a gear bag and an erotically sadistic turn of mind. Nick was different. He was mature, confident and sexy, but also self-aware and sensitive to what made his partner tick. It made him not only a much better Dom, but a more compelling person.

Nick's eyes hooded in a sexy way as they moved over her naked form. Though she wasn't shy about her body, something in his gaze made the blood rush to her skin, warming her all over. But there was something else there — something more than just physical desire. Was her romantic heart running away with her, or had she seen a flash of real longing in his dark eyes? Not just longing for a hot scene he could have with any sub girl — but desire for a connection with *her*?

Did she even want that?

"*Yes*," a voice breathed fervently in her head. "*Yes, yes, yes.*"

"I just had an excellent idea," he said, turning back to his gear bag.

Facing her, he held up a pink rabbit vibrator still in its wrapper, along with the remote control that went with it. His smile was at once sensual and cruel. "I want to give you added intensity while you're in the vacuum bed," he said in a low, sexy voice. "I'm going to take you beyond every limit you thought you had."

His words were exciting. His dark, sexy tone made her catch her breath. "Yes, Sir," she breathed softly, transfixed by his fiery gaze.

She lay down on the platform, settling herself against the latex inside the rectangle of PVC pipes. She was both excited and nervous at the thought of being immobilized in latex, but the scales definitely tipped toward the excitement side.

Nick approached her and crouched beside her.

He held a hand towel, along with the vibrator and a tube of lube, his gear bag over his shoulder. He set down his bag, spread the towel on the floor and set the items on it. "Like I said, let's try out the pump first, just to make sure you're okay with the process. Place your arms at your sides and close your eyes."

He unfurled the clear latex and pulled it over her body, loosely covering her face. There was a hole already cut into the plastic, and he positioned it over her mouth. "You can use your safeword if you want—mercy, right?" As Sophia nodded, he continued. "You should be able to make sounds, but it can be kind of overwhelming with the pump going, so it might be easier to use a safe signal. Your signal will be to stick out your tongue and waggle it, okay?"

Sophia stuck her tongue through the hole and waggled it to show she understood. Her heart was beating fast, her nipples rising against the latex. She had no intention of using a safeword or signal, but recognized the need for one.

"Okay," Nick said. "I'm going to zip you up now. It's like a huge Ziplock bag. Close your eyes and purse your lips through the hole. I'll count down three, two, one and turn on the pump for a few seconds to see how you do."

He moved down to the base of the platform.

"Three, two, one." He flicked the switch. The engine hummed, sucking out the air around her body. The latex tightened around her, shrink-wrapping her like one of those vacuum-seal bags. The sensation was like nothing she'd ever experienced — full body bondage without rope or chain, her eyelids pressed closed, her nose and breasts flattened, her lips pooching guppy-like out of the latex. She sucked in air experimentally. She felt at once utterly helpless and deliciously cocooned.

Nick flipped off the machine, releasing the vacuum seal. He unzipped the top sheet and pulled it away. "How was it?"

She breathed a sigh. "Awesome," she proclaimed. "I think I'm in love."

"With me or the machine?" he teased.

Before she could answer, he said, "Just kidding. Let's do this thing."

He squeezed lubricant on the rabbit's phallus and the clit stimulator. "Spread your legs," he directed. He carefully inserted the penis-shaped dildo into her cunt and positioned the stimulator against her clit. "Close your legs and your eyes."

Sophia obeyed, incredibly aroused already.

Then, he repositioned the top latex sheet over

her face and body, the breathing hole around her pursed lips. Moving down to the pump, he flicked it on.

The air sucked away around her, sealing her inside the frame. It was like diving deep under water, everything muffled and at a remove. She startled when the rabbit whirred to life inside her. It was set at a low, steady thrum — not enough to send her too quickly over the edge.

Nick's hands were on her through the latex, moving over her shoulders, her breasts, her body and thighs… The sensation was both pleasant and odd. It was strange to be touched through the taut latex while sealed inside the airless bed.

The hands fell away, leaving her alone in the tight snug of the mummifying latex.

Then the thudding throws of a flogger thwacked against her groin, the sudden erotic pain juxtaposed with the pleasure radiating from inside her. The flogger flicked over her body without predictability. He covered every bit of her skin, from her shoulders down to her feet, each stroke sending her deeper into subspace. All the while, the vibrator at her sex thrummed and tickled.

Then, the sudden, sharp flick of a whip snapped across her right breast. It hurt just as much, if not more, than if it had been on bare skin. She yelped and jerked, though she wasn't able to do much more than wriggle slightly in the vacuum seal.

The vibrator ratcheted up in intensity, pulling a moan from her lips. Then the whip landed again, this time on the other breast. The tip caught her nipple in a blinding flash of raw pain that eclipsed the aching pleasure in her sex.

Then, all at once, something was covering her mouth. It took her a fraction of a second to process that it was his hand. The palm pressed firmly against her lips, completely cutting off her ability to draw in even the slightest gasp of air.

She wriggled beneath him, startled at this turn — something they hadn't negotiated in advance. Her heart pumped hard, pressure building behind her face. The toys at her sex filled her and vibrated against her in a continuing spasm of raw pleasure.

Don't panic, a voice in her head whispered. *You have your safe signal. He will feel your tongue against his palm. He will stop.*

The hand remained, covering the lower half of her face. A second hand circled her throat, tightening just beneath her jaw. Terror spurted through her veins, turning her blood to ice. Her heart was booming in her ears, her body trembling and twitching beneath the latex. Yet, she didn't push the tip of her tongue up through her lips.

In that moment, she understood that she trusted this man — this man she'd only known for a few days — more than she'd ever trusted anyone. She trusted him — quite literally — with her life.

Her body stilled its trembling. Her heart ceased its thrashing. Peace moved over and through her, covering her like a shroud…

All at once, the hand was withdrawn.

The world clicked back on.

Instinctively, Sophia sucked in a bushel of air through her pursed lips. The hum of the pump once again filled her ears. The toys pulsed deliciously at her sex. Hands moved seductively over her latex-wrapped breasts.

After a moment, the hands were gone, replaced by the thuddy swish of the flogger. She was cocooned in her vacuum-sealed cage, the slick cover of latex holding her down, the flicking kiss of the stinging leather, the raw, pulsing throb of the dildo and the sweet, insistent tickle of the clit stimulator combined in sensation overload like nothing she'd ever known.

She had moved beyond language, her mind blank, her body rigid and trembling. She had been reduced to pure animal — grunting and writhing in her confines. Her heart was pounding, her clit throbbing, her breath a ragged pant through forcibly pursed lips. She heard a high-pitched, keening wail over the hum of the pump's engine as her body hurtled into a powerful, obliterating climax…

The sudden silence yanked her back to awareness. A moment later, the latex was pulled away. The cool air instantly chilled her sweat-soaked body. She opened her eyes, squinted as they adjusted to the light.

Nick was leaning over her, his dark, lovely eyes moving over her face. "Hey, you," he said gently, concern etching his features. "You okay?"

She opened her mouth to speak, but only managed a croak. He slipped a hand under her neck and helped her to lift her head.

"Wow," she managed, a smile lifting her lips of its own accord as tears slipped down her cheeks.

"Wow, wow, wow, wow, wow."

Nick smiled. "I take it that's a yes?"

Chapter 6

Sophia lay on the recovery couch, a small, dreamy smile on her face. Nick gently smoothed balm onto the welts he'd painted over her breasts and upper thighs through the latex. He glanced at her face as he worked. He was startled to find her regarding him with studied intensity, as if memorizing the planes and angles of his face.

He cocked an eyebrow. "What?"

"Nothing," she said, flashing a dimpled smile. "Or, no. Everything."

"Everything?" he repeated, bemused.

"That was," Sophia said emphatically, "without a doubt, the most intense, all-encompassing scene I've ever been in. When you put your hand on my mouth"—a shudder moved through her at the memory—"I was both terrified and exhilarated. I felt so—so…" She seemed to be struggling to find the word. "So alive," she finally finished.

Nick smiled as he tucked an errant curl behind her ear, warmth flooding his soul. "You were incredible, Sophia," he said sincerely. "Your emotions were so raw — so palpable. I felt like I was there experiencing it with you."

He closed his eyes a moment, visualizing her trapped and writhing beneath the latex. When he'd blocked her ability to breathe, and then placed his hand on her throat, he'd straddled the high wire of risk-aware consensual kink, barely keeping his balance. How far could he have taken her? The raw power that had surged through his being as he'd held her life in his hands lingered even now in the form of a hard-on still pulsing at his groin.

"It's good that you had the presence of mind to stop when you did," Sophia said, as if reading his mind. "Because I honestly don't know if I would have stopped you. Being held down, sealed in, completely helpless… It was so *thrilling*. I really think I might have just let you go on and on until — "

"No," Nick interrupted sharply, her fantasizing aligning a little too closely to his for comfort. One of them needed to have some limits, and he understood it was he, as Dom, who had that responsibility. "It was very intense for me, too," he added, modulating his tone. "There was a moment there where I had to pull myself back. To remind myself it was my job not just to give you the submissive experience you crave, but to keep you safe in the process."

Sophia nodded. "I know. I think that's why I was able to let myself go so completely. I knew you were there to keep me safe." She smiled like a trusting angel, her dimples beyond adorable.

Something clutched in Nick's heart—something unfamiliar and almost frightening, yet also welcome.

Sophia reached out her hand and touched his arm, her smile falling away. Fixing him with those big, blue-green eyes, she whispered, "I want you to make love to me."

Nick drew in a sudden breath, startled at her word choice. Was this the moment that would tip the balance of their relationship from scene partners to lovers?

Did he want that?

You're dying to fuck her. Stop obsessing over semantics.

Leaning down, he stroked another springy lock of hair from her face. "I want that too, Sophia. Very much. Let me just finish cleaning up here and then we can go to my suite."

They were quiet as they rode in the elevator. Sophia was once again dressed, her nipples perking prettily against her low-cut top, her sandals dangling from her hand. Perhaps feeling his gaze on her, she turned to him, smiling.

When he smiled back, she laughed. "Sorry. I can't stop grinning." She put her hands to her face. "My cheeks actually hurt from grinning so much. It's all these endorphins zinging around in my bloodstream. Totally your fault."

"I accept full responsibility," Nick said, laughing too.

Once in his suite, he went over to the mini-fridge that was nestled between the desk and a bureau. He'd left his phone back in the room on purpose, not wanting to be disturbed during their scene. Now, he had a sudden urge to check both his phone and laptop in case there were any messages or emails that needed handling regarding the Cabot deal.

Don't you dare, he ordered himself. No way was he going to fuck up with Sophia a second night running. Instead, he pulled out the bottle of top-notch champagne he'd ordered from the bar earlier that day. He turned to Sophia, who had flopped back onto the sofa with a languorous sigh.

"Care for a glass before I ravage you, sexy girl?" he asked with a wolfish smile.

"I'd love one," she replied.

He popped the cork and filled the two champagne flutes he'd also had chilling in the fridge. Taking his seat beside her on the sofa, he handed her a glass. They clinked lightly and drank.

"Yum, that's delicious," Sophia said with appreciation.

"It is good," Nick agreed, finishing his glass. "Care for another?"

Sophia shook her head. "Champagne goes right to my head." She set her glass down on the end table at her side. "What I could use is a shower. I feel sticky from sweating in that vacuum bed."

Nick, too, set down his glass and got to his feet. He held out a hand to help her up. "How about I'll join you?"

"You'd better," Sophia retorted with a laugh.

He took her into the bathroom, which included a Jacuzzi bath tub and a separate shower stall. He turned on the water in the shower. As it heated, they stripped off their things.

Nick's cell phone started to ring in the other room. He pressed his lips together, annoyed. Couldn't they leave him the fuck alone for one damn night?

"Do you need to get that?" Sophia asked, her tone neutral, her gaze elsewhere.

"Absolutely not," he staunchly asserted.

They stood together under the hot water. Nick brought his arms around Sophia. She was a full head shorter than he, and she rested her cheek against his chest as they embraced. After a while, he reached for the soap and gently lathered it down her back and rubbed it along her rounded ass cheeks.

She turned so she was facing away from him. She had two adorable dimples above her butt. He reached around her, massaging her breasts, arms and body with soapy lather. Finally, he rubbed the bar along the cleft between her legs.

Sophia leaned against him with a soft moan as he teased her sex with soapy fingers. But after a moment, she twisted so she was facing him. She reached for the soap he held in his hand. He let her take it from him.

She lathered his body with soap, walking in a circle around him in the large stall. Returning to face him, she dropped to her knees in front of him and took his erect cock in her hand.

As she washed his cock and balls, he groaned and took a step back. "Slow down, sexy girl. Let's take this into the bedroom."

"Works for me," she said with a saucy grin.

As they left the bathroom, Nick could hear the fucking cell phone again. "Excuse me a sec," he said. He strode into the living room, grabbed the phone and flicked it to silent without even looking at the screen.

Returning to the bedroom, he took a moment to admire Sophia, who lay naked on the bed, her skin pink and damp from the shower, her nipples fully erect against the mounds of her breasts.

Dropping the towel he'd wrapped around his waist, he lunged for her with a guttural growl.

~*~

Sophia held out her arms, pulling Nick over her. She loved the heavy feel of his body draped over hers. His cock was hard between them, trapped against her thigh. They kissed for several long, lovely minutes, their hands roaming over each other's bodies.

Her cunt ached to be filled, but she wanted to take her time. She wanted, somehow, to give him as much pleasure and satisfaction as he had given her during that intense scene.

Turning her face to break the kiss, she pushed at his shoulders. "Lie on your back," she whispered against his neck. "I want to suck your gorgeous cock."

He didn't need to be asked twice, but what man did? He rolled from her and lay on his back beside her, his erect shaft bobbing in the air like a divining rod.

Sophia scooted between his legs and crouched. She cradled his heavy balls in one hand as she lowered her mouth in a slow, seductive tease over him.

He moaned as she drew her lips along his length. She suckled him, using her tongue and throat muscles until he moaned again. Then she lifted her head slowly, releasing his shaft by inches until she held only the head between her lips. She watched his face as she teased the head of his cock and drew her tongue along its slit.

He stared back at her with a dark, intense gaze,

his lips softly parted. Reaching for her, he placed his hand on her head and slowly, sexily, forced her mouth down over his cock until she again took him to the hilt.

He entwined his fingers in her hair, twisting a handful and tugging lightly. Using her hair, he pulled her head up until his shaft nearly fell from her lips. Then he pressed her down again, controlling her movements until her nose was pressed against his pubic bone, his cock lodged deep in her throat.

She'd planned to take control, but he'd once again asserted his dominance. And she *loved* it. She adored the sense of erotic helplessness as he forced her head up and down over his cock. Her nipples ached and her clit throbbed.

All at once, he pushed her away and flipped her onto her back. Climbing over her, he reached for her wrists. Pulling her arms up, he pinned them to the mattress as he forced her legs apart with his thigh.

Then his cock was at her entrance. She groaned, arching her hips to take him inside. "Yes," she begged, barely aware she was speaking. "Yes, yes, yes..."

When he entered her, her cunt spasmed around his cock in a paroxysm of pleasure. He moved in a sensual circle inside her, the head of his cock catching that sweet spot as he swiveled. She moaned, straining against his grip on her wrists, delighted that she couldn't escape.

He brought her to the edge of a climax and then, all at once, stilled. "Not yet," he murmured throatily in her ear. "We're going to take our time." Lifting his head, he sought her mouth with his. His lips were soft and warm over hers, his tongue insistent. They kissed for a long while, his cock still hard as steel inside her.

Eventually, he pulled away and stared down at her with a look of such tenderness it took her breath away. Letting go of one of her wrists, he stroked her hair from her face. "Sophia," he murmured. "I…"

He didn't finish the thought, instead lowering his head again to kiss her mouth as he again reached for her free wrist, pinning it once more to the bed. He moved inside her, thrusting hard, his skin hot against her. His cock was again stroking her sweet spot from the inside out and this time he didn't stop when she tensed and trembled beneath him, balanced on the edge of a climax.

"Oh, god, oh, god," she cried as tremors of pleasure racked her body.

Letting go of her wrists, he slid his hands

beneath her and rolled to his back, taking her with him, his cock still buried deep inside.

She lifted herself into a sitting position astride his hips, her hands resting on his shoulders for support. He reached for her breasts, cupping them. Then his fingers found her nipples. He rolled them, each sensual caress making her nerve endings sing with pleasure. Then he twisted sharply, the erotic pain shooting directly to her cunt, which spasmed around his shaft.

"Take the pain," he growled in a low, sexy voice. He twisted harder, his fingers tight around her throbbing nipples. "And give me the pleasure." He lifted his hips, thrusting even deeper inside her.

She responded in kind, swiveling and grinding her splayed cunt against his pubic bone. It was all so perfect—his cock filling her, the throb at her clit as they moved against one another, the perfect erotic pain at her breasts as he twisted and teased.

"Oh, god, oh, god," she chanted again as waves of pleasure rose higher and higher inside her.

Nick was breathing hard now, his eyes fixed on her as he thrust upward to meet her gyrations. His hands fell away from her breasts, reaching for her hips. "Yes," he hissed, moving her back and forth over him. The perfect friction against her clit drove her nearly out of her mind as she orgasmed against him with a protracted cry of raw pleasure.

The tendons on his neck stood out, his color high, sweat on his brow. "Fuck, yes," he panted, jerking against her. "Sophia. Oh, Sophia..." The words were like a caress.

He stiffened suddenly and then spurted in a hard spasm inside her. His movements sent a series of climactic aftershocks through her frame, making her shudder and gasp as she fell forward against him.

Strong arms came around her, enfolding her in a warm embrace. Nick rolled to his side, taking her with him so they lay face-to-face on the bed, arms and legs wrapped around each other, his perfect cock still inside her.

They lay quietly for a long while as their breathing slowed and their bodies cooled. Sophia drifted in a quiet, warm place, her body sated, her mind pleasantly empty. What a lovely way to fall asleep...

Eventually, Nick pulled away from her. Gently, he pushed the hair from her eyes. "Sophia?" he asked softly, pulling her from a light doze.

Reluctantly, she opened her eyes.

Nick had lifted himself on one elbow. He regarded her with a cocked eyebrow.

"Hmmm?" she asked lazily.

"Don't even think about going to sleep," he said, chuckling. "Now that we took the edge off, I'm going to take my time. I'm going to make love to you all night long."

Sophia briefly thought of protesting. She was tired — exhausted even — from the amazing events of the evening. Yet, his words had reawakened her body, which tingled all over with anticipation. She couldn't seem to get enough of this guy.

"What the hell," she said with a laugh and a toss of her head. She opened her arms to receive him. "Sleep is for the meek."

Sophia squinted into the pale lavender pre-dawn light that washed the room. The bed was empty beside her. For a moment, she had no idea where she was. Then, she remembered.

"Nick?" she called softly, assuming he must be in the bathroom.

Speaking of which, she needed to pee. She threw back the covers and padded to the toilet. The ambient glow of a large nightlight was enough to see by, but the room was empty. Where was Nick?

She peed and then splashed water on her hands and face. She returned to the bedroom, where there was still no sign of him. More awake now, she stepped into the living room.

Nick was at his desk in a pair of shorts, his broad back bare. "I get it," he was saying quietly but urgently into the phone. "Brian... Brian, stop it. Calm down. It's going to be fine. I'm sure we can... No. I told you, I'll be there when —"

"Nick?" Sophia asked softly.

Nick whipped around in the chair. "Sophia," he said, clearly startled. She could hear a masculine voice talking loudly and urgently through the phone. Frowning, Nick said, "Brian. Brian, stop a second. Hold on. Listen, I'll call you back. No. I promise. I'll call you *right* back."

He pressed a button on the screen and set down the phone. He smiled at Sophia, though the smile didn't reach his eyes. "I'm sorry. Did I wake you?"

"No," she replied, wrapping her arms around her torso, suddenly cold. "At least, I don't think you did. I woke up and you weren't in the bed, so..."

"Yeah." He shrugged apologetically. "I couldn't

sleep so I got up and made the incredibly stupid mistake of checking my cell phone. We've still got some funding issues and Brian is going berserk." His phone buzzed on the desk. He placed his hand firmly over it.

"It's bad, huh?" Sophia commiserated. "I assume this is the same deal that's been distracting you since you got here?" She strove to keep her tone neutral and kind. It was clear that whatever he was dealing with was upsetting him—and his business partner—quite a bit.

"Yeah," he admitted with a sigh. "I may have to"—he broke off, dragging a hand over his forehead and pushing back his hair. "Fuck. I hate this. But I'm afraid…" He looked up at her, his eyes beseeching. "I'm afraid I'm going to have to cut my vacation short. This deal is going to completely fall apart if I don't get back there and do some hands-on damage control."

Sophia's first instinct was to wail, *Noooooooo! You can't go, you bastard. Not now—not when something amazing is happening between us.* She bit back the words, reminding herself they'd known each other for what – three days and change? She had no claim on Nick however amazing their time together had been.

He was a work-driven guy who placed his

career above everything else. That was starkly clear at this moment. And who was she to blame him? She ran her own business too, albeit on a much smaller scale. She knew there were times when only your presence would do, no matter how much support you thought you'd put in place.

Be a grown up, she counseled herself as she struggled to swallow her bitter disappointment. *He feels bad enough…*

"Hey," she managed, pushing her mouth into something she hoped approximated a smile. "I get it. You've got to do what you've got to do. Maybe we can reconnect at some point. Once I'm back in the city and once you've put out all your many fires…"

Nick rose from the desk and moved toward her. He took her into his arms. She held herself stiff at first, unable to settle into his embrace. But she relented as he held her close, stroking her hair as he murmured, "I'm *so* sorry, Sophia. Thank you for understanding. And, yes. Definitely. We'll definitely reconnect once you get back."

She let him kiss her, but something inside her heart—a window that had been opened for the first time in a long while—slid silently closed.

Chapter 7

Sophia punched in the keycode beside the glass door of her small Brooklyn apartment building. The actual flight time to JFK from Norfolk, Virginia, the closest major airport to the Outer Banks, had been under two hours. But she'd been traveling for over twelve, including the boat from the island at seven that morning to Hatteras, the two and a half hour shuttle ride to Norfolk, the wait time in the airport, the crush of people at JFK, the air train to the subway and finally, the subway's R train to the 36th Street station.

Juggling her bags and the flowers wrapped in newspaper she'd bought on a whim from a street vendor, Sophia fished for her mailbox key in her purse. She'd forgotten to put her mail on hold before leaving for vacation. The tiny mailbox was crammed with junk mail wedged in so tight she had to use two hands to get it out.

Laura, her assistant, as well as her best friend,

had kept everything running smoothly at the shop while she was gone. But there was something wrong with the point of sale equipment that needed to be addressed right away. And several large boxes had just arrived from Sophia's last scavenging trip to various estate sales in upstate New York. She was excited to see the pieces again, some of which she'd gotten for far less than they were worth. She couldn't wait to get them all cleaned up, priced and out onto her tiny showroom floor. Sophia had been planning to stop by the shop on her way home, but she'd been too beat.

"Don't worry," Laura had said, a smile in her voice when Sophia had called on her walk from the subway station to her building. "It'll all still be there tomorrow. Get a good night's rest and I'll see you in the morning. I can't *wait* to hear *all* about your kinky adventures."

Laura, who was in her late twenties and recently married, wasn't actively into BDSM. But she was aware of and completely comfortable with Sophia's kink. She had even gone with Sophia to a BDSM club a couple of times, mostly to gawk. And she had recently confided that she and her new husband, Ben, had added what they called "BDSM lite" to their sexual repertoire, including fuzzy wrist cuffs and playful spankings.

The tiny elevator was out of order, as usual, so Sophia trudged up the four flights to her apartment. She unlocked and opened her door. Edging past her bicycle in the narrow front hall, she dropped her bags to the floor with a relieved sigh.

The building she lived in was nothing to write home about, with its crumbling red brick façade, tiny front lobby and perennially broken elevator. But she loved her apartment, most especially because of the light. The place had surprisingly large windows, set so she got both the early morning and afternoon light. She'd reupholstered some wonderful Art Deco armchairs and a loveseat in a lovely pale lemony yellow floral that always made her smile.

Heading into her kitchenette, she pulled out two vases from the cabinet. She arranged the pretty white and yellow hydrangeas she'd purchased and brought them back out to the living room. The air was stuffy, despite the central air the landlord had recently put in. The sun hadn't yet set so she opened a window, letting in the sound of children playing, hydraulic breaks squealing, honking horns and a siren in the distance.

It was quite a contrast to the peacefully breaking waves and seagull cries she'd enjoyed over the past week on the island, but she loved the sounds of the city just as much, if not more.

And Nick lived only a subway ride away.

For a sudden, insane instant, she very nearly turned around and dashed out the door. They'd exchanged contact information and she'd looked up his address — a swanky, doorman-attended building near Central Park. She could call for an Uber and be there in under an hour.

Except that he wasn't there.

She pulled her cell from her bag and read his text message again, just in case she'd gotten it wrong. But no. The words hadn't changed.

"Hey, there. I know we were planning to meet as soon as you got back. Unfortunately, I have to fly down to Houston tomorrow. I've finally got this deal back on track, but there's a venture capital group down there I want to meet with face-to-face before I bring them onboard. I should be back early tomorrow evening. I can't wait to see you, sexy girl!"

She'd resisted the urge to retort something extremely snarky, instead only replying, *"Good luck with your venture capitalists."*

But now, alone in her apartment, she didn't have to hide her true feelings. She didn't need to put on a brave face or pretend she was as cool with all this as Nick seemed to be.

But underlying the frustration, her heart actually ached with the absence of him. She pressed her hand to her chest, as if that would ease the pain. She'd let down her guard, and Nick had come tumbling into her life, whether she wanted him there or not.

During their insanely brief but passionately intense connection, she'd finally found someone she could trust, totally and completely. He not only understood her need for dark, edgy erotic intensity, he embraced it along with her. Even within the BDSM scene, that kind of connection was as rare as hen's teeth.

Now she was forced to ask herself—was what they'd shared something that could only exist in the rarified air of a place like Desire Island? Could that sort of intensity and passion continue now that they were back in the real world?

It takes two, Sophia, a voice whispered in her head. *If you shut him out — if you're too afraid to take the chance, then you'll definitely be left with only memories.*

Sophia sighed. The little voice was right. But it wasn't only up to her.

Following Nick's departure, the rest of her vacation had played out well enough. She'd refused to sulk. Instead, she'd flung herself into various seminars, especially enjoying the BDSM yoga relaxation and positions classes offered by a lively, friendly staff slave called Abbie. Though Sophia wasn't at all flexible or particularly graceful, when she took the classes with the serenely smiling Abbie, she'd been able to fully relax, putting all thoughts of Nick aside, at least for that hour. And she'd had one more surfing lesson, which had been fun. She'd actually managed to stand up on the board, even if it had been for less than three seconds.

She'd gone to the dungeon parties each night as well, engaging in casual scenes with guys whose names she forgot almost before she knew them. While none of the scenes came close to the intensity of experience and passion she'd found with Nick, she'd managed to enjoy herself, more or less.

Nick had texted her perhaps a dozen times since he'd left the island. It was mostly sexy banter, mixed in with his continued apologies for cutting his vacation short, and excitement at seeing her again. She'd texted back light, breezy responses. She'd kept her stronger feelings under wraps, both the positive and the negative.

They hadn't spoken on the phone, though he'd called and left voice messages a few times. Several times she'd picked up her phone, her fingers poised to return the calls, but she hadn't followed through. She'd been afraid her anger would come out, and she would start making demands on a man who, despite their astonishing connection, she really had no claim on.

Now, she went into her bedroom, most of which was taken up with a wonderful Henredon dark ash sleigh bed she'd found at a barn sale in Pennsylvania Dutch country. Though she was in desperate need of a shower, the bed was calling her name, with its brightly patterned Mennonite patchwork quilt and pile of down pillows.

Giving in to temptation, she flung herself onto the bed with a contented sigh. There was nothing like your own pillows on your own bed, especially after having been away. She closed her eyes and fell almost at once into a deep sleep, too exhausted even to dream.

~*~

Nick had been working pretty much nonstop since he'd returned to New York, trying to salvage the teetering Cabot deal. Brian's inability to cope on his own had made some things clear to Nick, not so much about Brian but about himself. While he'd brought Brian in with the intention of making him a full-fledged partner, he'd always held such tight reins on the business that Brian hadn't really had a chance to get his feet wet and his hands dirty. With Nick always right there, he wasn't used to handling crises on his own.

Now, finally, it looked like the deal was back on track, but at what cost?

The prospect of losing a deal wasn't one he had been willing to entertain. His priority had always been business first, pleasure second. When he'd cut his vacation short and hightailed it off the island and away from Sophia, he hadn't really considered the potential repercussions.

In the past, if a woman he was dating balked and hit the road because his work obligations got in the way of their relationship, he would shrug and move on. He was too busy to spend his time trying to win back someone who didn't want to be with him on his terms.

He had, he was beginning to understand, always taken the women in his life for granted. Whatever compromises had to be made were made by them. It hadn't mattered that much to him before.

But it mattered now.

Sophia had seemed to be understanding about his need to salvage this deal. But he'd sensed the coolness of her texted responses and was keenly aware she hadn't returned his phone calls. He'd promised himself he'd make it all right when she got back. He'd planned to surprise her by being at JFK, a huge bouquet of flowers in his hand, when she returned that evening.

Instead, he was sitting on a plane, heading in the wrong direction. He waved away the airline attendant's offer of another scotch and soda. "What the fuck am I doing?" he muttered to himself as the plane descended. He glared out the window at the thick bank of clouds that hung over Houston like a shroud.

You're clinching the deal. You're going to be a million dollars richer once you finally put this one to bed.

Again, he wondered, at what cost?

It wasn't like he needed the damn money. And if that deal had fallen apart, there would be other ones — probably better, less risky ones.

But there wasn't another Sophia.

He'd never met anyone like her — someone who so perfectly fit his groove. The time he'd spent with her, albeit brief, was like nothing he'd experienced before. She was this amazing combination of strong, independent, free spirit and delicious submissive masochist. She could keep up with every dark fantasy he entertained, pushing his limits along with her own. It was exhilarating. Everything about her was just right. And he had a million diabolically wonderful ideas in mind for when they got back together.

He was beyond frustrated about the unexpected trip to Houston. He couldn't wait to see Sophia again. He would repair whatever damage had been done. He would make it up to her. That was a promise—both to her and to himself.

~*~

The next morning, having slept like a log for ten hours straight, Sophia awoke at dawn. She sprang from the bed, excited at the prospect of heading over to her shop. She had been so exhausted the night before, she hadn't even brushed her teeth. She headed into her bathroom—the room so small she could barely close the door once she'd maneuvered herself inside—to use the toilet and wash up.

As she lathered her hair under the invigorating hot spray of the shower, she couldn't deny the swoop of excitement at the thought of seeing Nick again.

Hurrying with the rest of her shower, she grabbed a towel, gave herself a cursory drying and, towel wrapped turban style around her head, went in search of her phone. Pulling it from her purse, she saw she had two text messages from Nick.

"A quick meeting and then I'm heading back to NY. I have plans for you upon my return."

"Oh, you do, do you?" Sophia said aloud, excitement again overriding her misgivings.

"My flight is scheduled to arrive at 6:24. See you around 8? I want to take you to Impulse, one of my private members-only BDSM clubs."

A jolt of excitement shot through her at the thought of seeing Nick again in a few short hours. She'd heard about but never managed to wrangle an invitation to any of the various private BDSM clubs that dotted Manhattan. Going with Nick to one of *his* clubs would definitely be the icing on the cake.

A cold, stubborn part of her tried to hang onto her anger at his leaving Desire Island mid-way through their passionate adventure, and to remind her that Nick was trouble. But she could already feel that part of her melting. The truth was, she couldn't wait to see him again, whatever the terms.

Still, she didn't want to make it *too* easy for him. He'd have to work, at least a little, to get back into her good graces.

"Sounds like fun," she texted back neutrally. *"Where should we meet?"*

Almost immediately, the little dots started undulating on the screen, indicating that he was typing. *"I'll pick you up at your place. I'll text when I'm close."*

"See you tonight!" She added a heart emoji, deleted it, added it back, and hit send.

"Welcome back," Jane, the barista at Sophia's favorite coffee shop said as she came up to the counter. "The usual?"

"Yep," Sophia replied, passing over her insulated travel mug. "Thanks."

Jane fixed a large regular coffee with steamed heavy cream and placed it on the counter. As she turned back to prepare Sophia's bagel with lox, cream cheese, onion and tomato, she said, "You look so tan and rested. Beach vacation?"

"Outer Banks of North Carolina," Sophia replied, smiling back.

"Oh, I've always wanted to go there," Jane replied. "Which island did you stay at?"

"Kitty Hawk," Sophia lied, not sure how Jane would take to the idea of a resort island dedicated to BDSM play. Not wanting to compound the lie, she said instead, "Those blueberry scones look good." She pointed to the tray of fresh scones on the counter.

"Just came out of the oven," Jane said. "Want a few for later?"

"Absolutely. I'll take four."

Slipping the food into her backpack, Sophia waved at Jane, who was busy helping a group of six teenagers who had just noisily entered the coffee shop, no doubt on their way to school.

Outside, the sun's rays were just peeking over the Manhattan skyline in the distance. While the air was humid, it was still cool and pleasant at that early hour. Sophia placed her travel mug in the cup holder, unlocked her bicycle and slipped the heavy chain into the saddlebag on the back. Easing the bike onto the designated path near the curb, she pedaled down the block to *Sophia's Treasures*.

Unlocking the front door, she pushed it open, causing the hanging brass bells to tinkle in welcome. Flicking on the lights, she stared around her shop with delight and contentment. She had missed the place, with its eclectic assortment of fine antiques and funky junk, liberally interspersed with curios and the knickknacks her aunt Lenore had called *tchotchkes*. She closed her eyes, inhaling the welcoming, familiar scents of lemon oil, wood polish, lavender and sandalwood, with undertones of mothballs and musty leather-bound books.

It was only a little after seven, and the store didn't open until ten. She walked her bike through the shop to the back room. She'd suggested Laura take a well-deserved day off, but Laura, being Laura, had replied, "Are you kidding? I'm still waiting to hear every delicious detail of your vacation!" Which was why she'd bought the scones — Laura's favorite.

Sophia, nearly done unpacking, cleaning and cataloging her new arrivals, looked up at the sound of the tinkling bells at the front door. A glance at her watch told her it was a little after nine. "That you, Laura?" she called out.

"One and the same," Laura called back.

She appeared a moment later, two large to-go coffees and a greasy white bakery bag in her hands. "I bet you've been here since five a.m., am I right? You were probably in antique withdrawal, having been forced to spend a whole, entire week relaxing on a beach all day and playing in kinky dungeons all night. You must have been going insane," Laura teased as she handed Sophia one of the coffees.

"You have my number," Sophia agreed with a laugh. She set down the cup to give her friend a big hug. "I have to confess, I didn't obsess about the shop quite as much as you might think. I was, uh, pretty distracted—at least for the first half of the week."

"So, tell me all about this guy you met," Laura said excitedly. "You've been dropping hints about this sexy dude all week. That's why I'm here early. Stop what you're doing right this second and take a coffee break. I brought apple turnover donuts from Moe's to celebrate your return."

"Yum," Sophia enthused. "And I brought blueberry scones from The Bean."

"My absolute favorite," Laura said, rubbing her hands together.

They went into the tiny kitchen just off the back room and sat at the two-seat teal Formica table, circa 1950, Sophia had unearthed from her grandmother's cluttered basement.

As they ate and sipped, Laura peppered Sophia with questions about Nick. While she didn't go into great detail about the intense BDSM scenes, Sophia did share that they'd had an immediate and intense attraction that only increased each time they connected. She had already told Laura about his bailing early, and how disappointed she was.

"But you're seeing this Dom again soon, right?" Laura asked eagerly. "The romance will continue?"

A wide grin broke out on Sophia's face, despite her best efforts to remain cool, calm and collected. "I hope so," she said.

"What do you mean, you hope so? Sounds like a match made in heaven. You guys are perfect for each other."

Sophia sighed.

"What? What's the sigh about? What's the problem here, girlfriend?" Laura spoke in a teasing way, but Sophia could see the concern in her eyes.

"It was amazing while we were together, but was it just a heat of the moment thing? Something that could only happen in that kind of perfect BDSM environment? Was it like Vegas? What happens on Desire Island stays on Desire Island? Because, the truth is, Nick is a workaholic. And like any addiction, it can tend to override everything else."

Laura snorted. "Look who's calling the kettle black? Sometimes I think you should put a cot back here. You're here seven days a week."

Sophia shook her head. "It's different. I love

what I do, but I can put it aside. When I was on the island, I knew you were here taking care of things, and honestly, I barely thought about the place. But Nick..."

She paused, reliving for the thousandth time the pre-dawn morning after the best sex of her life, when Nick turned from his desk, his face a study in regret. And while she understood the decisions he'd had to make, there was no getting around the fact that he'd chosen his work over her.

"Nick lives, breathes and *is* his work. I'm not sure he can have a separate life. At the same time, he is reaching out so... So, yeah — I'm willing to see him again."

"You're *willing* to?" Laura's comically skeptical expression made Sophia laugh.

"Okay, okay," Sophia admitted. "I'm *dying* to. But I have to be careful. I have to remind myself we don't really know each other all that well. I'm not interested in setting myself up for heartbreak. I refuse to be one of those women who pine after a guy who isn't available, for whatever reason. I'm thirty now, Laura. I'm too old for that shit. When I fall in love this time, it's going to be for keeps."

"I get it," Laura said, placing a sympathetic hand over Sophia's. "But we don't always get to pick how we fall in love. Sometimes it just happens. You step off that cliff and *wham* — you're falling, whether you like it not."

"Yeah, I know." Sophia sighed. "That's what I'm afraid of."

Chapter 8

Sophia finally finished closing the last of the dozen or so hooks down the front of her waist cincher. She regarded herself in the mirror with satisfaction. The cincher gave her a sexy hourglass figure, along with a nice breast lift. Her crazy curls had decided to obey for once, and hung in pretty ringlets down her back.

She had chosen a black leather skirt with a slit along one thigh. She drew the line at uncomfortable shoes, however, and had opted for her Doc Martens instead. The combination of sexy sub girl and kickass street fighter pleased her. She grinned at herself, eager anticipation at seeing Nick again zipping through her veins.

It was odd she hadn't heard from him since before he had boarded his flight in Houston, but maybe he'd just been too busy and distracted — or too intent on coming straight to see her!

He was due at her place in a half hour or so. In

spite of her promises to herself to remain cool, she let out a little whoop of excitement.

Her phone rang — not the chime of a text, but an actual call. Nick! Maybe he was already downstairs on the street.

"Oh my god, oh my god, oh my god," she chanted as she raced to find her phone.

Grabbing it from the bureau, she saw the photo of Nick standing on the beach on Desire Island staring pensively out at the ocean — the only picture she had. She'd taken the shot after one of their long, lovely walks along the shore during their brief but intense time together. She'd added the photo to his contact information on her phone.

Now, she clicked on it with excited fingers.

"Sophia." His deep, sexy voice sent a zing of desire hurtling through her body. "Hi. I'm so glad you were able to pick up."

A stab of guilt poked her for not taking his previous calls. Why had she been so stubborn?

"Are you back in New York?" Sophia asked. "I'm all dressed up and ready to go. I'm wearing something sexy and new. I hope you'll like it."

"About that," he said slowly, his words and the

hesitant way in which he said them instantly dragging her down. He blew out a sigh while she braced herself. "I'm actually not in New York."

"You're still in Houston?" she blurted, rising outrage threatening to push past the recent excitement. If he was still working on that fucking real estate deal…

"No, no," he said quickly. "But here's the thing. An older gentleman had a heart attack back in coach. They had to do an emergency landing in Ohio. He's apparently going to be okay, but I have no idea when we're getting the hell out of here. We've been sitting on the tarmac at the Columbus airport now for over an hour. You know how they do—first they say they expect it'll just be a short delay, and we'll soon be in the air and making up for lost time, yadda yadda. Then ten minutes becomes twenty. Then the gate they thought they had is no longer available, etc. I know you were really excited to go to Impulse tonight, and I was too. The thing is, I have no idea when I'm getting back to the city, or how long it'll take me to get to you once we do land. It's not fair of me to expect you to wait around. I was thinking—if you want, I can have my driver pick you up and you can go to the club without me. You know—just to check it out. I could let my manager there, Elizabeth, know you were coming and make sure you get the royal treatment."

Sophia thought about it for a second, but a second was all it took. "No," she said staunchly. "I don't want to go to your club without you. That would totally suck."

She drew in a deep breath and let it out slowly as she tried to corral the jumble of her feelings — deep disappointment that their reconnection was to be delayed yet again, irrational fury directed toward the poor man who had suffered a heart attack, less irrational fury at Nick for having left town in the first place, and annoyance with herself for wanting to stamp and shout and hold her breath until she turned blue unless she got her way.

"Listen," she continued, forcing herself to speak like a calm grownup, even though she didn't feel like one at that moment. "It's not your fault. It's nobody's fault. Maybe I'll just shuck the leather and stay in. Make some popcorn and watch an old movie."

"I hate to think of you doing that, especially when you're already all dressed and ready to go," Nick replied, urgency in his tone. "I feel really rotten this happened. I'd feel even worse if you opted for old movies on TV instead of some intense sensory deprivation or at the very least a nice hard spanking. Please, Sophia. I know you well enough to know you have needs that shouldn't go unmet for too long."

"I don't know," Sophia said, wavering. In point of fact, she had been going through BDSM-withdrawal since leaving the island. Not to mention, she was having an excellent hair day, and it would be a shame to waste such a rare opportunity to show the world.

"What about that place you were telling me about? The Den? You could go there. Just to have a nice, stress-reducing session. It would make me feel better, knowing I hadn't completely destroyed your evening."

"I don't know," she said again. She'd have to take two different subway trains to get there, and, especially dressed as she was, she wasn't sure that was a good idea.

As if reading her mind, Nick added, "I'll send my driver to take you. You just have to text him when you're ready to be picked up. His name is Samir and he'll be driving a silver Audi A8. I'll send him your contact info and he'll text when he's outside your building. Okay?"

Nick sounded so hopeful and so sweet that Sophia couldn't refuse him. Not to mention, it would be kind of fun to be driven from Brooklyn to Midtown by a driver—how fancy!

"You've talked me into it," she said with a

laugh. Her anger had melted away, though the disappointment remained.

"Just one thing," Nick added.

"What?"

"Don't fall for anyone."

Samir drove her in style in Nick's luxurious sedan to The Den, which was housed in the basement of a swinger bar in Midtown. The walls were painted black, the space dimly lit by sconces with bulbs that wavered like candlelight. The place was dark and edgy, the players more hardcore than what you found at the typical slap-and-tickle clubs that comprised most of the NY BDSM club scene.

Sophia paid her cover and entered, stopping just inside to scope things out. A man and woman stood at attention on the small stage at the back of the room, hands behind their heads. They both were naked, save for gold body paint from the neck down. A guy dressed in black leather and a black captain's cap moved behind them, flicking a whip over their glittering bodies.

The bondage wheel—the Den's coolest new piece of equipment—was occupied, of course. Because of its novelty and popularity, the club had started using a signup sheet for twenty-minute slots, with a ten-minute cleanup in between. The sheet always filled up within moments of the club's opening, and Sophia had yet to try it out.

People were scening at the other various stations set up around the room, or clustered at tables around the bar. Some couples were making out in corners. There was a guy with his pants undone, very obviously masturbating while watching one of the scenes.

For a moment, Sophia considered turning around and heading out the door. Samir was on call to take her home at the end of the evening—all she had to do was text. He probably hadn't even made it down the street yet.

While she desperately wanted to scene, this place was such a far cry from Desire Island. Damn it—had the resort ruined her for the regular clubs?

At the same time, her body reacted to the whistle of a cane, the moan of a sub, the slap of a hand against someone's ass. She'd come all this way. She'd stay at least a little while. It was crazy not to.

Sophia shifted the small gear bag on her shoulder as she scanned the room, looking for someone she knew. At that moment, there was a tap on her shoulder.

Turning, she looked up into the face of a Denzel Washington lookalike, circa 1992, and caught her breath. He was abso-freaking-lutely gorgeous. He wore a black T-shirt stretched over his muscular frame with the acronym RACK in shiny red letters that dripped as if with blood.

"Greetings, lovely lady. Care to engage in a little edge play? My name is Lord Brandon." He spoke in a rich, delicious British accent. Sophia had always been a sucker for British accents.

"Hi," she replied, trying not to gawk at his male beauty. The Lord title told her he was a Dom, though it also could indicate he was something of a poser. Not that it mattered — she was there to scene, not to judge. "I'm Sophia. I'm not sure I'm ready to scene quite yet. I just walked in the door."

"I saw you come in," he replied, flashing a brilliant, white-teethed movie-star smile. "I hurried over to claim you before another could. You're ravishingly beautiful, Sophia." He rolled the r in ravishingly like an actor on the Shakespearian stage. "And your name is as lovely as your form. Like Sophia Loren, that Italian beauty of yesteryear."

Yesteryear? Who used words like that? In spite of herself, Sophia laughed. The guy was too much. "Actually, I'm named after my grandmother, Sophie Weinstein from the shtetl," she couldn't resist quipping back.

"From the... what?" Lord Brandon looked confused, his regal bearing slipping a bit.

"Never mind," Sophia said, chuckling. What the hell — she had come there to distract herself. And she was unlikely to find another piece of eye candy as lovely as this one. The gear bag on his shoulder looked promising, too. Both a cane and a flogger handle stuck out of the open zipper. "What did you have in mind for a scene?"

"I have the bondage wheel in a few minutes. I'd love to strap you in, lovely lady, and have my wicked way with you."

Oooh! The bondage wheel. Yummy. And wicked way sounded good to her.

She smiled up at him. "All right, Lord Brandon. You've convinced me. Let's go."

They made their way to the bondage wheel station. The wheel was made of sturdy stainless steel with a large padded body rest at its center. A man wearing only a thong was strapped in facing forward, a zipped black hood completely covering his head and face. A woman resembling the actress from *Elvira, Mistress of the Dark*, was flicking a plastic beaded whip over his body. His skin, sheened with sweat, was mottled with small red marks left by the beads.

A timer dinged just as Lord Brandon and Sophia arrived. Martin, the assistant manager who also served as bouncer when necessary, appeared. "Time's up," he said to Elvira. "I'll help you get him down."

The Mistress unzipped and pulled the black hood from her sub's face. She smoothed his mussed graying hair and kissed him on the cheek, the tender, intimate gesture telling Sophia they were a couple. Together, Martin and she unstrapped the guy and helped him from the wheel.

As the couple slipped away, arms around each other's shoulders, Martin sprayed and wiped down the apparatus. He glanced back at Lord Brandon and Sophia as he worked, his face breaking into a smile of recognition.

"Hey there, Sophia," he said. "It's been way too long. Where the hell have you been?"

"Here and there," Sophia said vaguely, smiling back. "Lord Brandon here is signed up for the next slot. I'm excited to try this thing out."

Martin's eye moved to Sophia's temporary partner, his tongue flicking over his lower lip as a bulge appeared at his crotch. "Hellllllloooooo there, sailor," Martin cooed in a campy, exaggerated way. "*Don't* tell me you're pure het? I'll have to kill myself immediately."

To his credit, Lord Brandon didn't take offense, as some straight guys would. "Sorry, mate," he replied, flashing those blindingly white teeth. "I've only an eye for the ladies."

"And a Brit, too. Oh my *god*," Martin wailed theatrically, but he, too, was grinning. "Figures. All the cute guys are straight."

Sophia laughed. "Hey, that's supposed to be my line. All the cute guys are gay," she retorted. Turning to Lord Brandon, she added, "Present company excluded, naturally."

Martin shrugged. "The grass is always greener..." His cleaning done, he addressed Lord Brandon, his tone more businesslike. "You ever used the wheel before?"

"Not this particular one," Lord Brandon replied. "But I am experienced with bondage wheels."

"We had this one custom made," Martin said with evident pride as he stroked the rim of the large wheel. "All the straps are Velcro for quick release.

Feet go in the anti-gravity boots to hold the legs steady, and there's a footrest for comfort and stability. You can cuff her wrists at her sides or extended."

He paused in his explanation to ask, "Do you have your own cuffs? If not, they're available for purchase. For hygiene reasons, we require you provide your own."

"I've got my own," Sophia piped up. She reached into her gear bag and pulled out her favorite leather cuffs, their clips already attached.

"Of course you do," Martin said with a grin. "What was I thinking?"

He returned to his spiel. "There are six different attachment points to choose from. Once you've got her strapped in, push this lever here" — he pressed a lever at the base of the contraption — "to unlock the wheel and you're good to go."

He gave the wheel a demonstrative spin and then reengaged the brake. "You can strap her in facing outward or facing the wheel. Nudity is fine. I'll be back in twenty minutes to help with takedown and cleanup. Any questions?"

"We're good, thanks," Lord Brandon said. As Martin walked away, Lord Brandon turned to

Sophia. "Do you care to disrobe, my lady?"

"Indeed, I do, kind Sir," Sophia replied in her best attempt at an English noblewoman. Dropping the accent, she added with a grin, "How can I get a proper whipping with all this leather in the way?"

"My sentiments exactly," he replied, gifting her with another radiant smile.

She handed him her cuffs so she could strip. As he took them, their fingers touched and something electric sparked along Sophia's spine.

Pulling her hand away, Sophia bent down to undo her laces and remove her boots. Lord Brandon watched her, his heavy eyelids hooding as she unhooked her cincher and unzipped her skirt. Finally, she slipped off her panties. Folding her things, she placed them in her gear bag and set it aside.

"Safeword?" Lord Brandon queried, his eyes still flitting over her body.

"Mercy," Sophia replied, pleased he'd asked, not that she expected to use it.

He slipped the gear bag from his shoulder. "Whip, crop, flogger, cane? What's your pleasure?"

"I love them all. Surprise me," she said.

They decided she would face the wheel, arms extended. Lord Brandon held her arm supportively as she stepped into the leg supports and got her balance. As she leaned against the padded body rest, he strapped her into place. Finally, he wrapped her cuffs around her wrists and extended her arms, clipping them to the wheel so she formed a human Y.

Sophia's entire body tingled with expectation, while at the same time something heavy, dark and perfect settled in her soul. She adored the helpless, delicious feeling of being bound in this way. She was excited at the additional sensation promised by a turning wheel.

If only it were Nick standing behind her.

She heard the click of the wheel brake being disengaged. "Here we go," Lord Brandon said. "Let me know if it's too fast."

The wheel began to turn, taking Sophia along with it. It was sturdy and well-balanced, but she squealed nonetheless, startled by the shift in her center of gravity.

"All good?" Lord Brandon queried.

"Yes, thanks," Sophia replied, adjusting to the sensation.

Lord Brandon started with the flogger, nicely warming her skin. She sighed with pleasure as the stinging leather made her come alive. As he flogged her, he kept the wheel moving at a slow, steady turn. The feeling was both thrilling and disorienting.

Taking her at her word, he graduated from the flogger to a riding crop, smacking her ass and the backs of her thighs with strong, steady strokes that fired her skin and quickened her breath. Next came the whip, its sting sharp and sudden. All the while, she turned on the wheel, her hair falling into her face and away again as the wheel righted.

Her clit was throbbing, her nipples hard against the leather body rest. In her mind's eye, Nick was behind her. In a moment, he would drop the whip and press his naked body to hers. He would kiss her neck and whisper that he was proud of his sub girl for taking her whipping with barely a whimper. Then he would enter her from behind, at the same time slipping his hand around her body to find and tease her cunt while his cock filled her completely...

She was startled by Lord Brandon's voice in her ear. "You're taking quite a whipping, lovely lady. None of the usual squirming and squealing. You please me."

"It's awesome," she replied breathily. He was doing a good job. It wasn't his fault that he wasn't

Nick Kincaid.

"I'm going to lock the wheel now," he continued. "I want to use the cane. That work for you?"

"Yes, Sir."

He spun the wheel until she was completely upside down, which she hadn't been expecting. Locked in that position, the blood rushed to her head. Her sense of helplessness intensified. Unless she shouted her safeword, she was truly at this man's mercy.

The cane whistled and struck, leaving a line of searing heat across both ass cheeks.

Lord Brandon crouched beside her and murmured, "That good? You handle that okay? There's a lovely mark."

"More, please," she begged in a throaty voice.

He got to his feet and stepped out of her limited line of sight.

Another whistling stroke made contact just where her ass met her thighs. The pain was intense, but was instantly enveloped in the warm, buttery embrace of submissive need.

"More," she entreated, the word barely a

whisper.

He struck again, this time catching both thighs at once.

"Ah," she cried. Blood was pulsing at her temples, her hair hanging wild in her face, sweat breaking out beneath her extended arms.

When the timer dinged, it took Sophia a moment to process the sound. The cane fell away. The brake was released and Lord Brandon slowly righted the wheel until Sophia was again upright.

As the blood rushed away from her head, she was suddenly very dizzy. "Oh," she grunted as she regained her bearings. "Wow."

She heard Martin's voice behind her. "Hey. Nice marks, dude. You know your way around a cane, that's for sure." She felt a hand on her shoulder. "You good, Sophia? The handsome Brit treat you right?"

"I'm great," Sophia replied, still riding high from the endorphins released by the erotic pain.

"We'll just get you down from there so the next couple can take their turn."

They released her quickly and helped her from the wheel. "Aftercare is in that back room behind the stage," Martin said to Lord Brandon. Glancing at Sophia, he added, "She knows where it is."

Sophia crouched by her gear bag. Unclipping her cuffs, she dropped them inside and then unzipped the side pocket. She pulled out the knee-length cotton robe she had brought for the purpose and slipped it on.

"I've got a marvelous balm especially compounded by a chemist's shop I frequent in London," Lord Brandon said. He waved a hand theatrically toward the back of the club. "Lead the way, lovely lady."

Sophia allowed Lord Brandon to smooth the ointment, which smelled of lavender and eucalyptus, over her ass and thighs. As he worked, she said, "That was really a wonderful session, Lord Brandon. The wheel made it especially intense. Thank you for the scene."

"You're most welcome," Lord Brandon replied. "But we're only just getting started, I hope? Do you enjoy hot wax? Medical play? Or, we can cut directly to the chase. I have a delightful suite booked at the Four Seasons. It would be my pleasure to take you there and make love to you until sunrise."

Before Desire Island, Sophia would have agreed in a heartbeat to all of the above. After all, the guy was handsome, a skilled and attentive Dom, and she loved hearing him talk, even if the constant "lovely lady's" were a tad annoying.

Just then, she heard the faint but unmistakable sound of her cell phone dinging in her bag. Had Nick landed in New York? Was he, even now, on his way to see her? His image rushed into her mind's eye — his dark, lovely eyes, strong features and engaging smile. The warm curve of his body curled around hers their last night together, and that first time he'd kissed her on the beach under the sparkling stars...

"Sophia?" Lord Brandon prodded gently, his face quizzical.

"I'm sorry," Sophia said with a small shake of her head. "You were truly wonderful. But my heart belongs to another."

She'd used the line before as a way to let a guy down gently. But this time, as terrifying as it was to admit it, the words were true.

The next morning, naturally, Laura and Sophia dissected every detail of the previous evening with Lord Brandon. "Okay, I have to ask," Laura eventually said. "Where does Nick fit into all this?

How can you pursue true love with one guy while scening with another?"

"True love?" Sophia attempted a dismissive laugh but wasn't sure she'd pulled it off. "I've decided we're just friends with benefits. " Maybe if she said it aloud, she could convince herself it was true.

But Laura, who knew her better than anyone, did that nose wrinkle thing she did when she wasn't buying it. Before she could express her skepticism, Sophia added, "It's easy for you to talk about true love. You and Ben are perfect for each other. You've made the ultimate commitment with marriage. With Nick and me, it's different. We're still so new. We were together all the time at the resort because we were on vacation, and not just any vacation. Desire Island is the kind of place that fosters intense and immediate connections."

She sighed, missing their time on the island more than ever. "But now, back in the real world, things are more complicated. Nick's made it pretty clear that his business comes first and foremost. I need to be careful about getting too involved with a guy like that. He has so many irons in the fire that there doesn't seem to be a whole lot of time for anything — or anyone — else. I'm not ready to hand my heart over to someone who's only around every so often to accept it."

"Methinks the lady doth protest too much," Laura replied with a knowing smile.

Just as Sophia was gearing up for another defensive retort, her phone dinged with a text message. Glancing at the screen, she caught her breath. "It's Nick," she squealed.

Laura just grinned at her.

"Hey, sexy girl. Can I cash that raincheck tonight? Dinner and then a grand tour of my BDSM club? I have a surprise for you. You might want to review your safeword..."

Chapter 9

At Laura's insistence, they went shopping together after she closed the shop to find a new outfit for Sophia's date with Nick. The red silk cocktail dress Laura picked out wasn't something Sophia would have chosen on her own, but she had to admit, it was both sophisticated and sexy.

She was already waiting by the curb when Samir pulled up to her building that evening. Before the car even came to a full stop, Nick leaped out of the car to take her into his arms. As he held her close, something that had been curled tight inside her since they'd parted unfurled. It felt so *right* being in his arms. She could have stayed there forever.

When they eventually parted, he took a step back and whistled appreciatively. "You look stunning, Sophia," he said, his eyes moving hungrily over her.

"You don't look so bad yourself," she replied, beaming with pleasure at his compliment.

Nick was in a beautifully-tailored dove-gray suit, his shirt open at the neck, every bit the GQ gentleman. Settled in the back seat, they couldn't resist cuddling and kissing a little, in spite of Samir's presence in the front as he wove his way through the city traffic.

Nick took her to dinner at a small, elegant place where the menu had no prices and the ratio of wait staff to patrons was three to one. She would have found it pretentious, but the food and Nick's excellent company were so good she forgot to be judgmental.

When they exited the restaurant, Samir was idling at the curb, ready to whisk them to their next destination. Nick's club took up an entire four-story brownstone in a hushed, elegant neighborhood in Greenwich Village. You wouldn't even know the club was housed there, save for a discreet placard over the antique doorbell that read *Impulse – Private Club*.

"Whoa. This is stunning," Sophia enthused. "It looks more like a nineteenth century mansion than a BDSM club."

Nick nodded. "That's what it used to be, back in the day. Come see what we've done with it." He punched in a code on a pad beneath the doorbell and the lock clicked open.

They entered a large foyer, the floors of marble tile inlaid with beautiful mosaic patterns in turquoise and gold, a classic crystal, ten-candle chandelier sparkling overhead.

"Oh, Nick," Sophia breathed, awestruck. "This is exquisite."

Nick looked around, the proprietary pride evident on his face. "I wanted to create something different from the usual run-of-the-mill underground club. I wanted something elegant and private, dedicated to people serious about the lifestyle. This is a members-only club and all prospective applicants are vetted, much in the way they're vetted for Desire Island. We have a second location here in the city and a new one in Los Angeles that's doing very well. In fact, I'm thinking of expanding overseas. Maybe London? Paris? I haven't decided."

Sophia had understood Nick was wealthy, but she hadn't really grasped the scope of his wealth. These elegant clubs were just a side hobby he'd gotten into for fun.

In her admittedly limited experience with the truly wealthy, Sophia had found that they tended to believe their money gave them rights that didn't extend to the rest of the world. It was somehow understood that allowances had to be made for the sacred task of earning even more of the stuff. Unfortunately, Nick confirmed rather than dispelled that belief. He'd cut his vacation short in the name of closing a deal, derailing their newfound, intense connection in the process. And he'd broken his date with her, again in pursuit of the holy grail of cold, hard cash. How much more of the stuff did any one person *need*, for chrissakes?

An attractive woman came striding into the foyer. She was tall and stately, dressed in a black leather vest and matching leather pants. In her late forties, she had burnished chestnut hair swept back in jeweled combs, her lips painted a shiny red.

"Nicholas," she said warmly, moving toward him with outstretched arms. "We're so delighted you've come this evening. We've missed you terribly." As they embraced, she gave Nick air kisses on each cheek.

She let him go. "And this beautiful young woman must be Sophia, yes?"

"The very one," Nick agreed, beaming from one woman to the other. "Sophia, this is my good friend, Elizabeth Owen, manager of Impulse. Elizabeth, meet Sophia Weinstein."

"A pleasure," Sophia said, wondering if *good friend* was code for anything more, and then telling herself to cut it out. She had no exclusivity rights, through her own choice.

Elizabeth took both of Sophia's hands in hers. "I've heard wonderful things about you. I haven't seen Nicholas so smitten since..." She paused, furrowing her perfectly arched eyebrows. "Well, since ever, actually," she finished with a musical laugh.

Nick laughed, too. "Guilty as charged." He put his arm around Sophia, pulling her close.

Sophia leaned into him, feeling ridiculously happy and pleased, in spite of her promises to herself to keep her emotional distance.

"Is the room set up?" Nick asked Elizabeth.

"You betcha, boss," Elizabeth said with a conspiratorial grin. "Including a gear bag with the requested items."

"Excellent. Thank you, Elizabeth."

"The room?" Sophia asked, curious. "What room?"

Nick tightened his grip around her shoulders. "You'll see. But first, how about a quick tour?"

"I'd love that," Sophia agreed eagerly.

They stepped into an elegant living room furnished with fine antiques beautifully upholstered in silk and leather. Oil paintings were framed in gold gilt against cream-colored walls. People were seated here and there about the room. A man in black dinner jacket with jeweled cufflinks glittering at his wrists reclined on a leather divan, a naked woman kneeling on the carpet at his feet, her head resting on one of his knees. He was talking quietly to another man seated in an armchair across from him, a wineglass in his hand. He wore black leather pants and a red silk pirate's shirt, the laces opened to reveal tufts of gray curls at his chest.

In another grouping sat two women, both dressed in elegant designer suits and sophisticated gold jewelry, as if they'd come straight from Wall Street or a fancy law office. They were attended by very handsome, younger men, both in white shorts, their smooth, tan chests bare.

On closer inspection of the room, Sophia saw the St. Andrew's crosses, one on either side of an ornate Italian Renaissance marble fireplace. She noted the slave cages set at various intervals around the space, some tall and narrow, some long and low. Two of them were occupied.

A naked woman was inside a standing cage, her back to them, her fingers tight around the bars. Her bare bottom showed evidence of a recent, rather severe caning. The other, nude save for a leather harness and slave collar, was lying on a thick pad in a sleep cage, her eyes closed, a half smile on her face.

Neither Nick nor Elizabeth paid the slightest attention to them. "Along with its being an informal gathering place," Elizabeth was saying, "we hold slave auctions in this room. We also host the occasional party or wedding ceremony for those of our guests who like whips and chains as part of their festivities."

"And who doesn't?" Sophia couldn't help but quip.

"Indeed," Nick agreed with a laugh.

"Most of our play spaces are private dungeons available by appointment," Nick added as they walked through the room toward a wide, curving staircase of beautiful mahogany. "We also have bedrooms on the fourth floor for members who come in from out of town, or just want to stay overnight."

The second floor consisted of private dungeons with equipment to rival anything on Desire Island, with an added overlay of opulence. They were only able to view a couple of the rooms, as the others were occupied. Sophia was becoming increasingly aroused, both by the BDSM equipment with all its potential, and the sounds of snapping leather and cries of erotic pain from behind closed doors.

"Which room are we going in?" she pressed, curiosity getting the better of her.

"Patience is a virtue in a submissive," Nick teased.

"Good thing I'm not a sub," Sophia retorted with a grin.

Nick chuckled. "You're incorrigible."

Elizabeth bid them a good night as they ascended the stairs to the third floor. "The rooms on this floor are more specialized," Nick explained. "A hot wax room, a medical exam room, a cross-dressing room, a mirrored room with a suspension rack at its center so you can see and torture your slave girl from every angle."

"Oooh," Sophia breathed. "That sounds hot. We going there?"

"Nope," Nick replied cryptically. He led her past several closed doors to the door at the end of the long hall. "This is where we're going. I had it designed especially with you in mind. I haven't seen it yet, either. Hopefully, Elizabeth made sure all my specifications were met."

He opened the door and flicked on the light.

The space was a nearly exact replica of the vacuum bed chamber on Desire Island. It had the same counter at the back and recovery couch on a side wall. Just like the one at the resort, there was a vacuum bed set on a raised platform covered in black latex, a clear sheet of latex over the top. A small gear bag sat waiting nearby, as promised.

"Whoa," Sophia exclaimed. "It's like you airlifted this whole thing from the Outer Banks."

"I got the specs on the vacuum bed from the resort management, and sent them, along with a detailed description of what I wanted, to Elizabeth. She took care of the rest," Nick replied as he closed the door and turned the lock. "I'm thinking of adding a vacuum bed chamber in all my clubs."

"Cool," Sophia enthused, moving closer. Her juices were already flowing with anticipation. She couldn't wait for the intense sensory deprivation experience.

"For the next half hour," Nick said, "you will be my willing and compliant sex slave. Your first task is to strip and get on your knees."

"Yes, Sir," Sophia agreed willingly, her nipples hard against the black lacy bra under her red silk.

To her delight, Nick, too, removed his clothing. She admired his long, lean body as she stripped. His cock was already semi-erect. Her cunt tightened at the sight.

"On your knees," he reminded her in an imperious tone, his dark eyes hooding with lust.

She dropped at once to the yoga mat at his feet, her mouth watering with anticipation. She reached out, eager to cradle his balls and grip his shaft.

But he stopped her, placing a hand on her head. "No hands," he directed in a low, sexy voice. "Put them behind your back and keep them there until I direct you otherwise."

"Yes, Sir," Sophia replied, gripping her forearms behind her back with the opposite hand to give herself balance.

Nick reached for her hair, gripping a handful of curls in his strong fingers. He pulled her head forward, guiding her mouth to his cock, now fully erect. She parted her lips, savoring the sweet weight of his shaft on her tongue as it glided back until the head was lodged in her throat.

She closed her eyes as he thrust slowly in and out of her mouth, his fingers still tangled in her hair. It wasn't long before he was panting, his thrusts more insistent.

"Look at me," he commanded in a low, throaty voice. "I want to look into your beautiful eyes while I fuck your mouth with my cock."

A jolt of submissive lust hurtled through Sophia at his words, making her entire body throb with need. He locked his eyes on hers as he thrust in her mouth. She stared back, mesmerized as he gazed directly into her soul.

All at once, his body stiffened and, with a cry, he jerked forward, climaxing in a series of powerful spasms. Sophia did her best to swallow, startled by the suddenness of his ejaculation.

Apparently, he hadn't expected to come quite so quickly either, because he barked a laugh and said, "That caught me by surprise." He untangled his fingers from her hair and took a step back. "I guess it's a good thing. It'll take the edge off so I can take my time with you."

He held out his hand. Sophia let go of her arms from behind her back and allowed him to pull her upright. She couldn't help but grin, delighted that Nick had been so aroused that he couldn't contain himself.

"Lie down on the bed, sexy girl," he instructed,

leading her to the platform. "What I have in mind will make our previous vacuum bed session seem like vanilla missionary play. I'm going to take you further than you think you can go, and then just a little past that."

An involuntary shudder of nervous excitement passed through Sophia's frame. "Sounds kind of scary," she blurted, hugging herself.

He moved closer, standing directly in front of her. He placed a finger under her chin, forcing her to look up at him. His eyes were glittering, his lips lifted in a sensual, cruel smile. "A little fear is a good thing," he said in a soft voice tinged with steel.

Though she trusted him implicitly, Sophia swallowed hard, her mouth suddenly dry.

~*~

Sophia looked so sexy, her lightly tanned skin and pink nipples a pleasing contrast to the shiny black latex beneath her. They'd talked over dinner about their relationship going forward. And while Nick wasn't especially happy with her assertion that "friends with benefits" was the way to go, he wasn't in a position at the moment to press the issue.

It was ironic. He'd always been the one in past relationships to try to slow the tide of emotions. He hadn't wanted to get tied down to any one woman, especially given his rigorous work schedule and periodic need to travel. He'd even been thinking of suggesting to Sophia that they take their time, now that they were both back in the city.

But when she'd been the one to say, without a hint of anger or resentment, that she understood his work came first in his life, he'd very nearly argued that no, *she* came first.

Which was insane, given that they'd only known each other such a short time.

Though, as Elizabeth, a one-time lover and still a good friend, had pointed out once to him — BDSM relationships were like vanilla relationships on steroids. A first date involving rope and a flogger was, by its very nature, more intimate and intense than dinner and a movie.

Whatever happened going forward, he was super turned on at the moment, despite his recent orgasm. Already, his cock was tingling, his balls tightening in anticipation of what he had planned for her.

He reached into his gear bag and pulled out the small pillow he'd packed for the scene. "Lift your ass," he directed. "I'll want better access during this session than we had back at the resort."

Sophia looked confused. "But the latex," she began.

"This will be a little different than last time," he interrupted. "You'll see. Now, do as you're told."

Sophia obligingly lifted her ass, allowing Nick to slide the plump pillow underneath her, forcing her hips up.

"Good. Now, spread your legs as wide as you can while still keeping them on the bed. As she complied, he added, "You've already demonstrated you can take quite a lot. Tonight, I want to push you to the very edge. I want to test your limits of erotic pain and pleasure. Do I have your permission?"

"Yes, Sir," Sophia said, her eyes shining, her lips softly parted. "Yes, please, Sir," she added with a small, saucy grin.

Nick smiled back, his eyes narrowing with anticipation. "Excellent. I'm going to pull up the latex top sheet and zip you in place. There's already a hole cut for your mouth. Before I turn on the pump, I need to make a few additional alterations."

He pulled out a pair of scissors and a Sharpie pen. Sophia's eyes widened in question. Before she could ask, he said, "I want access to your pretty little cunt, not to mention those lovely nipples." He crouched beside her and pulled the latex loosely over her to mark the right spots. He drew strategic circles and set the pen aside. Lifting the latex sheet, he cut the holes he'd marked.

"Remember," he said as he pulled the latex sheet up over her body once more. "If you don't feel you can speak, your safe signal is to waggle your tongue. Got that?"

Sophia nodded, a combination of fear and excitement radiating from her in almost-tangible waves.

He placed a sleep mask over her eyes. "I'm going to seal you in now and turn on the pump." Getting to his feet, he zipped the latex closed around the perimeter of the bed. He adjusted the top sheet until the holes were properly aligned over her mouth, breasts and cunt.

"Stick out your tongue if you're ready to begin," Nick directed, his finger on the switch that would activate the pump.

Her pretty pink tongue appeared from between pouting lips.

He flicked the switch and the pump came to life. Its vacuum-cleaner hum filled the room as it sucked the air from between the layers of latex, effectively shrink-wrapping the naked girl.

He started at her breasts, which rose in luscious, rounded mounds above the latex, her nipples fully erect. He took two individual clover clamps from his bag. Pulling each nipple taut in turn, he pressed open the clamp and let it close again, catching and compressing each nipple in the process.

Sophia moaned through the aperture in the latex, the sound one of both pleasure and pain unique to sexual masochists. Satisfied with his handiwork, Nick retrieved the rabbit vibrator from his bag and crouched at the base of the bed. After lubing both the phallus and the clit stimulator, he eased the phallus carefully inside her and positioned the rabbit ears snuggly against her clit.

Getting to his feet, he took a step back to survey the lovely, bound girl. She looked phenomenally sexy—immobilized in latex, her nipples clamped, her cunt stuffed, her mouth in a pout as if waiting for a kiss. She was completely at his mercy, and he planned to make the most of it.

Returning the lube to the gear bag, he pulled out the rabbit's remote, along with his favorite single tail whip. He turned the remote to its lowest setting, causing Sophia to jerk beneath the latex. Taking a step back, he snapped the whip experimentally against her right breast, careful to avoid the clamp.

She gave a small cry as she registered the pain. A lovely red mark appeared where the tip of the leather whip had made contact.

He gave her left breast a matching mark and whipped his way along her torso and down to her mons. Then he turned up the remote a notch, pulling a sexy moan from his captive's lips.

Added pleasure called for additional pain. He snapped the whip against her thighs and the soles of her latex-covered feet. That got a strong response, as he'd known it would, her cry far louder than before.

He turned up the remote another notch to distract her, and then reached once more into his goody bag. He pulled out a very thin, whippy cane, perfect for marking tender breasts.

He whipped it in the air near her ear, curious if she could hear its whistle over the sound of the pump. Apparently, she could, because she reacted to the sound by tensing and emitting a small cry of alarm — or was it anticipation?

Setting the cane aside for the moment, he regarded her compressed nipples. While she could have withstood that particular torture longer since her nipples had surely numbed by now, he didn't want the clamps interfering with the cane.

Crouching beside her, he grasped each clamp between thumb and forefinger. He compressed the springs to release her nipples from their vise-like grip. As the blood flowed back, Sophia yelped, probably as much from surprise as pain.

He quickly cupped her breasts, gently massaging the nipples with his palms. Bending over her, he kissed and licked each tortured nipple until her cries segued into sighs of pleasure.

His cock throbbing, he picked up the cane again and flicked the whippy rattan rod against the creamy mounds, leaving narrow red welts behind. Unable to resist in any way, Sophia squealed and moaned in her latex body sheath.

With the pain came more pleasure. He turned up the rabbit another notch, and Sophia emitted a low, guttural sound, like a cat in heat.

Crouching at the base of the bed, he flicked the cane at her spread thighs as the vibrator pulsed at her cunt. As welts rose on her skin beneath the latex, he turned up the vibrator to its highest level.

Getting to his feet, he walked around the bed, flicking the cane over her immobilized form. Her nipples were hard as pebbles, her entire body trembling, a steady moan issuing from her lips. Sophia twitched and cried out at each cruel flick of the cane. At the same time, the vibrator was drawing her inexorably toward climax. Her moans and breathy sighs were like fingers massaging his cock. If he so much as touched himself, he would explode.

As he moved around her, he kept a careful eye on her face, listening for her safeword, watching for her safe signal, but Sophia held out. He'd never been with anyone before who could take as much as she could. She was fucking awesome.

The pleasure was now overtaking the pain. Sophia writhed beneath the latex, her orgasmic cry a keening wail. The cane fell from Nick's hand as he watched in admiration and delight. His cock was hard as steel, his own recent climax notwithstanding. He couldn't wait to make proper love to this sensual, responsive woman.

Deciding she'd had enough, he flicked off the vibrator and gently pulled it from her body. He considered climbing over her then and there. He would thrust himself into the hole he'd cut away while she remained captive beneath the latex, still wracked with post-orgasmic aftershocks.

But he wanted more than that with Sophia. He wanted more than to use her body solely for his own sadistic and sexual pleasure. He would take her up to one of the VIP bedrooms on the top floor of the club. There, he would make love to her. Slow, delicious, intimate love.

He flicked off the pump, releasing the suction that held her down. In the sudden silence, he asked, "You all right, Sophia?"

"Hmmm."

Nick unzipped the latex and peeled it back. Sophia's body was sheened with sweat, her cheeks flushed, her nipples still at full attention. He gently lifted the sleep mask from her eyes.

She squinted up at him with a sexy, sleepy smile.

"Hey, you," he said, a sudden tenderness nearly overwhelming him. What was happening to him?

Gently, he slipped an arm beneath her shoulders and helped her to a sitting position. As he tucked a curl behind one seashell pink, perfect ear, he asked again, "You okay, baby?"

"Oh, yeah," she sighed, still smiling that dreamy smile. Her blue-green eyes sparkled like sea glass. "Nick, that was *incredible*. Let's do it again."

Nick laughed, delighted with her. "Insatiable girl. I love that about you."

He helped her to stand and then took her into his arms. He placed his hand lightly on the back of her head as he pressed his mouth to hers. Her lips parted and he slipped his tongue past them as he pulled her into a close embrace, loving the feel of skin on skin. His heart actually hurt in his chest, aching with tenderness, while at the same time, his cock, pressed hard against her hip, throbbed with lust.

When they parted, she stared up at him with shining eyes. "Holy moly," she said with a breathless laugh. "The boy can kiss, too!"

With a joyous whoop, he lifted Sophia in his arms and carried her to the recovery couch.

As he settled her onto it, he said, "We'll definitely do it again, but you've had enough right now. Time for a little aftercare and then I'll take you up to one of the VIP suites for some champagne and..." he waggled his eyebrows suggestively, making her laugh again.

As she reclined on the couch sipping sparkling water, he smoothed a healing cream over the worst of her welts. Just as he was finishing, there was a sudden, sharp knock on the door.

Nick swung his head toward the sound, scowling with annoyance. Who the hell was that?

"Do we need to get that?" Sophia asked. "It

sounds pretty insistent."

"Fuck, no," Nick swore. "My staff knows better than to disturb me. It's got to be some new member or other who's confused. We'll just ignore it and they'll go away."

But the knocking continued, now accompanied by a masculine voice he recognized as Phillip's, Elizabeth's second in command. "Excuse me, Mr. Kincaid," Phillip called through the door. "I'm terribly sorry to disturb you, but there's an emergency at the other club. Apparently, the place is on fire. A four-alarm fire, sir," he added in an urgent tone. "Elizabeth felt you needed to be told at once."

"A fire," Nick cried. "Is anyone hurt? How did it start?" He had risen to his feet without realizing it. He glanced back at Sophia, who had lost that dreamy, satiated look.

She was regarding him with concern. "Pull on your clothes," she urged. "You have to go. Obviously, you have to go, Nick."

"I can't just leave you," he began, but she was already up too. She strode purposely toward his clothing and gathered it into a bundle. He glanced helplessly from her to the closed door.

172

Of course, she was right. He had to go. His people could be in trouble. Someone might be hurt. He had to get over there and see what was happening. While Sam, the manager at Impulse II, was good, he couldn't be expected to handle this all on his own.

"Okay, Phil," Nick called through the door. "I'm getting dressed. I'll be right out. Call Samir and make sure he's out front waiting when I get down there."

"Yes, Mr. Kincaid," Phillip replied, the relief evident in his tone. "Right away, sir."

Nick pulled on his underwear and trousers and slipped his arms into his shirt. He allowed Sophia to button it while he zipped his fly, buckled his belt and stuck his feet into his shoes, not bothering with the socks.

"I'm *so* sorry, Sophia," he said, running his hands over his face and up through his hair. "I hate to leave you like this. I had wanted to make this night really special. I—"

"Don't be crazy," she interjected. "You've got people and property to see to. I totally understand. If it was my shop on fire, you can bet I'd be out of here in a New York minute."

Relief flooded through him at her understanding, though the longing and remorse remained. "You're really something. You know that?"

"So, I've been told," Sophia replied with a sassy grin, though something in her face had closed — her eyes no longer directly meeting his. "Now, get the hell out of here. I'll clean up."

He started to protest, to explain staff would take care of that, and that he would call her a cab or she could sleep upstairs, but before he could speak, she said urgently, "We'll talk later, Nick. This is an emergency. Do what you have to do. Go."

She turned away suddenly, but not before he saw the tears fill her eyes, one spilling down her cheek.

"Sophia," he cried, moving toward her.

"No," she said sharply, her face still averted. "I'm fine. I promise. You need to get the hell out of here. They're waiting for you."

Knowing she was right, and not knowing what else to do, he turned on his heel and went.

Chapter 10

Nick stared at the column of numbers. They stared back at him, stark and black against the light of the computer screen, their meaning suddenly indecipherable. It was two in the morning. The whole fire mess had put him seriously behind with his other projects. Not to mention Brian had just given his abrupt notice the day after the fire, leaving stacks of unfinished analysis and paperwork for Nick to juggle, along with everything else. Margery, his very reliable and much over-worked office assistant, had stayed until nearly nine every night since Brian had baled in an effort to help get things back under control. But Nick felt as if he were swimming against the tide — and being pulled slowly out to sea.

It wasn't long ago that he would have taken these various setbacks in stride. Nothing got Nick Kincaid down. Give him an obstacle and he'd find a way around, over or through it. He thrived on challenge and adversity. But lately, the game had lost its glitter and all he felt was exhausted.

Not to mention, he was in the process of letting the best thing — the best person — ever to happen to him slip through his fingers and, very possibly, out of his life for good.

"What the fuck are you doing, Kincaid?" he said aloud, pushing back from his desk with disgust. Since when had money and power become more important than love?

But that wasn't really the question, was it? The real question was, how had he lived his entire life before Sophia doing that very thing, and having no problem with it?

Though he was presently spending practically every waking hour trying to keep his business ducks all lined up and paddling nicely, his heart wasn't in it. In fact, it was nowhere nearby, which might explain why he was having so much trouble getting things done.

That drive — that obsessive, do-anything-for-the-deal drive had been derailed by this amazing woman who had exploded into his life that first day at Desire Island. She had remained front and center in both his heart and mind ever since then, but he'd been too busy to show her the attention and love she deserved.

He kept drifting into sexy daydreams about Sophia at the most inopportune times. Earlier in the week, he'd actually lost the thread of the conversation during an important conference call with several key players. He had trouble mustering enthusiasm for potential new deals that would have totally energized and absorbed him before he'd met this astonishing woman.

He hadn't seen her since the night of the fire, in spite of his best intentions. He simply had too much on his damn plate. Each night, when he finally found the time to call Sophia, she was always gracious, sexy and responsive. Yet, underneath her charm, he sensed she was slipping away from him. He was losing her.

And for what? Another piece of real estate? Another couple of zeroes on his bank balance?

Exasperated, he turned off his computer, not even bothering to save what he'd been working on. "This is fucked up, Kincaid," he said, pushing back from his desk and getting to his feet. "Something's got to change, and it's got to be you. And it's got to be now."

All at once, he knew what he had to do. The realization exhilarated him. The solution was so simple. The actual execution would be a little more complicated, but that was why he had lawyers and accountants. Once he'd made the decision, the rest was just details.

He laughed aloud and actually did a little impromptu jig right there in the office. It was as if he'd just thrown off a ten-ton weight he hadn't even realized he'd been carrying. He slipped his hand into his pocket, wanting to text Sophia his exciting news.

But he caught himself. It was the middle of the night. He wouldn't disturb her. Nor would he tell her what he *planned* to do. He would just do it. And then he would tell her, face-to-face.

~*~

Friday night, six days since the fire at Nick's club, Sophia sat in the back office closing out the accounts. Once she was done with that, she'd tackle pricing the new items she'd accepted on consignment.

She looked up in confusion when the brass bells on the front door tinkled, as she'd closed up the shop an hour earlier.

"Yoo hoo," Laura's familiar voice called out. "You still here, Soph?"

"Back here," Sophia replied. "What're you doing here? Did you forget something?"

Laura appeared at the doorway. "You."

"Huh?"

"I've come to collect you. You've been moping around all week. I'm not buying your 'everything's fine what are you talking about' line for another second."

When Sophia started to protest that everything *was* fine, Laura held up a hand.

"Don't forget—I've known you a long time, and I know when you're full of shit. So, put away whatever you're working on. It's been a billion years since we had a girls' night out."

"What about Ben? An hour ago you couldn't wait to get home."

Laura slapped her forehead. "I know, right? I totally forgot Ben had this bachelor party thing. I'm on my own tonight. I'm assuming, based on the moping, that you are, too?"

"I have *not* been moping," Sophia asserted, though maybe she had been—just a little. "And I'm on my own because that's what works for me right now, okay?" She could hear the defensiveness in her tone. Forcing a smile, she added, "Really, everything is good. We're just taking a little breather. Nick has a lot on his plate right now."

The fire had damaged a significant portion of the other club before it was contained but, fortunately, no one had been hurt. Still, there was plenty for Nick to deal with, including his partner's sudden defection, which only piled more on his already full work plate. Mindful of the pressure and stress he had to be feeling, Sophia had done her best to be patient and understanding. But the truth was, she was dying to see him, and if he'd so much as crooked a finger in her direction, she'd have come running.

"Okay," Laura said, her tone dubious. "If you say so." She put her hands on her hips and cocked her head. "So. We going or what? I'm starving. I'm thinking sausage, mushroom, peppers and onions. Oh, and some of those yummy garlic knots Sal makes. And a pitcher of ice-cold beer. You in?"

Sophia chuckled, aware resistance was futile. Laura had that determined "I'm on a mission" look that brooked no refusal. Not to mention, pizza and a beer sounded pretty darn good at the moment, as she'd worked through lunch.

"Okay, you've sold me." Sophia pushed back from the desk and picked up the security deposit bag. "We just need to swing by the bank on the way."

A half hour later, they were seated at a small table in the tiny neighborhood restaurant, each with a mug of beer on the red-checkered tablecloth between them. "What's the latest with the fire situation?"

"Nick's still dealing with the insurance company. They haven't yet ruled out arson, even though Nick says it's pretty clear it was an electrical issue."

"So, when do the two of you connect again? Sounds like your last date was awesome, at least while it lasted."

Sophia had told Laura about Nick's private club and had shared a broad overview of their hot scene, though she hadn't spent too much time on the details, which would freak out her BDSM-lite dabbling friend.

Sophia shrugged. "No firm plans at the moment. We'll probably reconnect soon. Maybe this coming weekend." She shrugged again, feigning nonchalance. "I don't know."

Laura regarded her with a quizzical expression. "You sound kind of lukewarm about seeing him again. Is the bloom already off the rose?"

Sophia was saved from answering as the

waitress arrived, carrying a huge pizza and a basket of garlic knots. The pizza looked fabulous and smelled wonderful. Sophia selected a piece and sprinkled it liberally with freshly grated parmesan and red pepper flakes. She added several buttery garlic knots to her plate and tucked in.

They ate and drank for a while in companionable silence. Then Laura, who would keep at something like a dog with a bone, said, "Back to Nick. I could have sworn you were falling in love with that guy. But now, I don't know what's going on. I just know you seemed down all week, even though you keep denying it." She placed her hands flat on the table and leaned forward. "Level with me. Tell me what's really going on in that head of yours. Are things cooling off between you?"

Sophia took a long pull on her beer as she thought about how to answer. This was Laura, after all — her best friend. She would just lay it out there — her endlessly looping conversation with herself — and see what Laura made of it.

"Here's the thing," she said. "I'm still completely obsessed with the guy. I think about him constantly. I get all shivery remembering our time together." She hugged herself, her body tingling with the muscle memory of being held down, the latex anchoring her in place, never knowing where the next stroke of the cane might fall. The erotic pain had been perfectly juxtaposed by the relentless intensity of the vibrating toy at her sex. But the experience had been so much more powerful because of their emotional connection. It had added a whole other dimension to their scenes, one she had never experienced with any other Dom.

"It's not just the sex," she said aloud. "Or even his incredibly intuitive knowledge of what I need. We had fun just walking on the beach, or sharing a drink at night by a fire pit. He makes me laugh. He's funny and kind. He cares about the people who work for him and provides benefits and health insurance to all his employees, even part-time ones. And the way he kisses..."

Sophia sighed, her fingers fluttering to her lips as she recalled their last, passionate kiss, their naked bodies pressed together. She would have melted to the floor if he hadn't held her tight in his warm, strong embrace. And then the dashing way he'd scooped her up in his arms as if she weighed nothing, like something straight out of a romance novel.

Laura laughed, cutting into Sophia's daydreams. "You should see your face. You've got it bad, girlfriend. You can spout all that friends with benefit nonsense till the cows come home, but any idiot can see it's more than that."

Sophia wrapped her arms protectively around her torso, her resolve stiffening. "No. This is the way it has to be. Friends with benefits is the only way to go with a man like Nick. There's a reason he's forty years old and still single. He's married to his career. Everything else—every*one* else—comes second by definition."

Laura looked skeptical but Sophia barreled on. "As hot, sexy, intense and perfect for me as he is when we're together, Nick Kincaid is not relationship material. And I have no intention of putting my heart out there to be smashed—not out of cruelty, but out of neglect, however benign and well-intentioned. I'm not some swooning teenager pining by the phone. I've got my own life to live. So, yeah—it's all good. I'll keep my options open. There are still plenty of Doms in the sea. It's all for the best. I'm good with this."

Laura eyed her for a long moment, doing that disconcerting thing she did where she peered directly into Sophia's head. "Whatever you say, chief," she finally said.

In stage whisper, she added with a sly grin, "Liar, liar, pants on fire."

~*~

Nick woke energized and excited on Friday morning, despite having had only five hours of sleep. He was still firm in his resolve to make some dramatic changes in his life, and determined to make it happen sooner than later — today if possible.

He looked at his phone in case Sophia had texted him, but the screen was blank. He opened the message app, but then closed it again.

He spent the next ten hours straight on the phone and in meetings, only taking a break when Margery forced him to eat a sandwich and get outside for a few minutes of fresh air. Of course, it would take time to actually seal the deal, but he now had the workings of a positive arrangement that would profit everyone involved. More than that, it would set him free.

He was aware that Sophia closed her shop at six and lived within walking distance of her business. He hadn't yet been to either her shop or up to her apartment, though he had been outside the building when Samir and he had picked her up.

It was just a little after seven when Samir dropped him at the curb in front of her building. He hadn't seen Sophia in six days. He hadn't told her he was coming. He wanted it to be a surprise —

hopefully a good surprise.

"I'll text in a while to let you know if I'll need you again tonight," he said to Samir as he gathered up the items he'd purchased. He flashed a grin, adding, "If things go well, I won't need you until tomorrow."

He juggled the large shopping bag and flower box into one hand as he punched in the four-digit code Sophia had shared with him that would gain him access into the building. When the buzzer sounded, he shouldered his way into the small, rather shabby lobby, which was deserted.

He walked to the single elevator and pushed the button. He took a step back and waited, bouncing nervously on the balls of his feet.

The elevator wasn't making any noise and there were no lit numbers indicating movement of any kind. That was when he noticed a placard lying on the floor near the elevator door. It had apparently fallen from where it had been taped, and read: **Out of Order** in bold printed letters. Beneath it, someone had scrawled in ink, *Again*.

With a sigh, Nick headed toward the stairwell. He climbed the four flights, gifts in tow. As he neared her floor, his heart picked up its pace, not out of exertion, but excitement. He walked down the narrow hall, past the sound of a baby crying in one apartment, someone playing loud music in another.

When he came to Sophia's number, he stood outside the door a moment, listening for sound. What if she had someone else in there? He should have called first. Or at the very least, texted. Well, it was too late now. He was here. And if he didn't see her soon, he would explode.

He pushed the doorbell and heard it ring inside the apartment. He held his breath, listening for the sound of her footsteps. But there were none. After a minute or two, he pushed the bell again, a little more insistently. Still nothing.

He took a step back, pondering what to do. He glanced at his watch. Maybe she had stayed a little late at her shop with a last-minute customer. Or maybe she'd stopped on the way home to pick up dry cleaning or some groceries.

He set down the bag and placed the flower box carefully on top of it. Leaning against the wall, he crossed his arms and settled back to wait.

Ten minutes passed. Then twenty. Nick slid down to the worn carpet and rested his back against the wall, legs extended, his eyes fixed on the stairwell door. After fifteen more minutes had gone by, Nick forced himself to admit that Sophia

187

probably wasn't coming home any time soon. For all he knew, she had already been to her apartment and gone out again. At this moment, she could be engaged in a hot scene at that club she liked to go to — The Den? Or, she might be out with some other guy. Or worse, at his place, in his bed…

Stop it, he admonished himself. Whatever she was doing, it wasn't really his business, even though he'd like it to be. He'd agreed with her friends-with-benefits arrangement when she'd proposed it. It had seemed like a good idea at the time.

Now, he could admit, at least to himself, it was the worst idea ever.

Hopefully, that was all about to change.

Reaching into his jacket, he pulled out his card case and removed a business card. Taking out his pen, he wrote on the back, *I have some news I want to share. I need to see you. Love, Nick.*

He positioned the bag and flowers in front of the door. Hopefully, no one would steal the gifts, but if they did, they did. He slipped the card just under the flower box ribbon and turned back for the stairs. He would find a pub or something nearby and settle down to wait. He wouldn't check his work email or the balances in his various investment accounts. He wouldn't call his attorney or his accountant for updates on their progress.

He would simply sit and wait.

There was nothing more important right now than waiting for Sophia — nothing at all.

~*~

Sophia climbed the stairs, thumbing through the flyers and junk mail as she moved toward her floor. It had been good to hang out with Laura over pizza and beer. She would have been happy to stay out longer, but Laura had needed to get home. Maybe, now that it was the weekend, Nick would finally have time to get together.

If he didn't, she'd go to The Den tomorrow night. She absolutely, positively would *not* become one of those women who pined after some guy. No way. Not happening.

She saw something in front of her apartment door as she made her way down the hall. Curious what it might be, she walked faster. "Whoa, what's this?" she breathed as she got to her door.

There was a long, narrow box wrapped in a red satin ribbon. It sat on top of a large white shopping bag with sturdy handles. She plucked out the small card stuck just under the red ribbon and read it.

"Nick," she exclaimed aloud. "Nick was here."

When she'd given him her building code, she'd had fantasies of his showing up in the middle of the night and swooping in to have his dark, evil way with her. That had yet to happen, but clearly, he'd remembered the code.

And now, he had news. He needed to see her. How mysterious!

She unlocked her door and gathered up the things he'd left for her. Inside, she moved through her tiny apartment and sat on the sofa, placing the items on the small coffee table along with her purse and the junk mail. First, she plucked at the ribbon and opened the box. She drew in her breath as she took in what had to be easily two dozen of the most beautiful, perfect long-stemmed red roses she had ever seen. She lifted one of the roses to her nose. The fragrance was fruity and delicate. The base of the stem was nestled in a rubber-tipped floral glass water vial, as were all the roses in the box.

She set the stem carefully back into the box and peered into the large shopping bag. She pulled out two bottles of *Veuve Cliquot* and a ridiculously large box of chocolates with *La Maison du Chocolat* stamped in black letters on the lid.

"Holy shit," she breathed aloud. "What's this all

about? Did he just close another insanely profitable real estate deal? Maybe buy a small country? Or is he just feeling guilty for being too busy to connect face-to-face for the past several days?"

Whatever his reason, that chocolate was calling her name, in spite of the earlier pizza and beer. Unable to resist, she pushed off the brown ribbon wrapped around the chocolate box and opened the lid. The most heavenly scent of rich chocolate assailed her as she stared down at row upon row of beautifully-made candies. She picked up one and took a bite, moaning aloud with pleasure as the rich, velvety flavors burst on her tongue.

As she chewed, her eye fell again on Nick's card. When had he come by? Why hadn't he called or texted?

One way to find out.

Fishing her phone from her purse, she started to text, but then decided against it. Even if the news was going to be bad, he deserved a call for the lovely gifts. She licked her lips as she waited for the call to connect, savoring the last bit of chocolate on her tongue.

Nick answered on the first ring. "Sophia?"

"Hi," she replied. "I just ate the best piece of

chocolate I've ever had in my life."

"Ah, that's a relief," he said. "I was worried someone might take the stuff."

"Nope. I'm looking at a couple dozen of the most beautiful roses I've ever seen, along with those awesome chocolates and two bottles of champagne. Now, all I need is the guy who brought them."

"I'll be right there. I'm down the block at a pub. I was waiting for you."

"Why didn't you text? Laura and I were having pizza at a neighborhood hangout. I could have met you."

"Doesn't matter. I'll be there in ten minutes," he said, sounding a little out of breath, as if he were already running toward her.

"Okay," she replied. "I'll leave the door…" She didn't finish the sentence, realizing he'd already clicked off.

"Curiouser and curiouser," she murmured as she stood to put the flowers in a vase and the champagne into the fridge.

It occurred to her then — she still didn't know if his news was good or bad.

Chapter 11

Nick raced up the four flights of stairs, his heart pounding. This was it. This was the moment when things either soared or plummeted between them.

When he got to her apartment, he started to ring the bell but then saw the door was ajar. Giving it a push, he said, "Sophia?"

"Come on in," she called.

He squeezed down a narrow entrance hall containing a bicycle, a backpack and a pair of sneakers. He stepped into a small but very nicely appointed living room. The roses stood in a blue glass vase on a small, octagon-shaped table beneath a large window. He could see what must be the bedroom through an open doorway.

"Back here," Sophia said.

Following her voice, he moved toward a rice paper screen. Behind the screen was a tiny kitchen with barely enough space for the top-freezer refrigerator and a two-burner hotplate and microwave set on the single counter. The box of chocolates was on the counter too.

Sophia stood at the sink, her long, curly hair hanging in ringlets down her back. She turned as he stopped in the doorway. She wore a long, colorful tunic, her feet and legs bare. She grabbed a towel to wipe her sudsy hands and held out her arms to him, her face dimpling in a wide smile.

"There's my prince charming — my bringer of chocolates and champagne, the perfect finish to sausage and onion pizza."

Laughing, Nick went to her, taking her into his arms and kissing her for a long time. She kissed him back, her hands circling his neck as he held her close.

When they parted, she looked up at him. "I can't take the mystery another second. What's all this about?"

"I have good news. Exciting news."

In spite of this declaration and his firm belief it was true, a stab of anxiety poked at Nick's gut. He didn't want to put pressure on Sophia by giving her the impression he'd done this for her. Yes, she'd been the impetus in highlighting the emptiness of a life lived only for work, but he'd done this for himself — for his own sanity.

He noticed the two champagne flutes drying on the rack beside the sink. "How about let's pop a cork and have a glass?"

Sophia flashed a grin. "You're determined to make me wait, huh? This is worse than waiting on the sequel after a really good cliff hanger," she teased. "But, okay. I'm not one to refuse a glass of good champagne."

He had to step out of the tiny space so she could open the refrigerator door. She took out one of the bottles and handed it to him. Picking up the two glasses, she said, "Let's walk the three steps from my vast kitchen to my huge living room."

"I love your place," he said sincerely, following her to the couch. "It's got a certain quirky charm."

"Thanks. I think," she replied with a chuckle. "As long as you're not claustrophobic, it's a great place to live. I love this neighborhood."

Nick peeled the foil from the cork and untwisted the metal housing that held it in place. Holding the bottle away from her, he popped the cork. He filled the glasses and handed one to Sophia.

She lifted it in a toast. "To friends with seriously

excellent benefits," she said, her eyes twinkling.

They clinked glasses and sipped. Nick drew in a breath, ready at last to fully speak his mind. "That's the thing," he said, turning toward her on the sofa. "I don't want that. Not anymore."

"You don't want the benefits? Or to be friends?" she replied, that impish grin again on her face.

He set down his glass and took hers, too, gently from her hand. "Sophia," he said. "I've sold my business."

She looked at him a moment without appearing to comprehend. "What?"

"The real estate development business. The deal isn't quite final, but I've got several buyers very interested and I'm definitely moving forward with this."

"Okay," she said slowly. "That's good, I guess?" She made the sentence a question.

"It's very good," he said emphatically. "It's what I want. I'm done working 24/7. I want more in my life."

Nick waited for more of a reaction. While he hadn't necessarily expected her to leap to her feet and squeal with excitement, he'd hoped for more than her somewhat bemused response.

He leaned toward her, speaking from his heart. "I didn't do this *for* you, Sophia, if that's what's freaking you out. I did it for me. Meeting you — connecting with you — has made me reexamine my priorities. I've come to realize that my life has basically been one non-stop workday. I'm never not working. And for what? I have plenty of money. All the money I need and then some. I have my BDSM clubs, and I have plans to develop more. But, for the first time in my life, I want more than just work." He took a breath, and then said the real thing — the main thing. "I want you."

Sophia got to her feet. But instead of moving closer and falling into his arms, she turned away. "I need chocolate," she said, heading toward the kitchen in almost a run.

Nick rose too, following her, uncertain what was happening.

Her back was to him in the kitchenette, the lid of the chocolate box now open. Apparently sensing his presence behind her, she said, "I'm sorry I'm being so weird. I think it's really great you're examining the priorities in your life and making positive changes. It's just... I'm not entirely sure what this means — for us."

Nick moved closer, placing his hand lightly on her shoulder. "Sophia, we're both old enough and have been through enough to know when something is real. And this is real. And I don't want to keep fucking it up by not being there. Yeah — when we're together, the sex is hot and the BDSM play is off the charts. But I want more than that. Relationships need nurturing and attention to grow. Don't think I'm not aware of how often I've let you down, even in the short time we've known each other."

Finally she turned to face him. "So, you're saying you're ready for more than friends with benefits?" Her smile was tentative — hopeful?

"That's exactly what I'm saying," he replied, taking both her hands in his. "Though our BDSM play has been seriously incredible, it's no longer enough to just scene with you and then fuck you. I want to make *love* to you. I want to go to sleep with you in my arms. I want to wake up with you next to me in the bed. I want to go grocery shopping with you. I want to travel with you. I want to stay home with you. I want to go estate sale hunting with you. I want to see your shop and meet your friends."

"Nick," she said softly, her eyes shining.

"I've always held myself back," Nick continued, needing for her to understand. "I told myself it was because I had no time for a relationship. But the truth was, I'd never found *the one*. And now I have. You're the one, Sophia." His voice cracked with emotion.

He was done being careful. His heart was hers, and he had to let her know, in no uncertain terms. "I love you, Sophia," he declared. It was the first time he'd said the words aloud. They were the truest words he'd ever spoken. "I want you in my life. I want you as my partner, with everything that entails."

He forgot how to breathe as he waited for her response.

Her eyes were luminous with tears. Taking his face between her hands, she stood on tiptoe and kissed his lips. The tears brimmed over and rolled down her cheeks. "Nick," she whispered. "Oh, Nick. I love you, too. I've loved you from the first day we met." Her arms circled his neck, pulling him down for a proper kiss.

As he held her, losing himself in her taste, touch and scent, his heart lifted, bubbles of joy popping inside him like the finest champagne. As they kissed, he lifted her into his arms. Her legs wrapped around his waist as he carried her from the kitchenette, through the living room and into the bedroom.

They fell together onto the bed, still wrapped in each other's arms, their kisses increasingly ardent. Nick's cock had morphed into an iron bar in his trousers. His hands roamed hungrily beneath her tunic. His fingers found the clasp of her front-closure bra and he popped it open so he could cup her lovely breasts.

She moaned against his mouth as he rolled her nipples. Dominant lust heated his blood, and he twisted her nipples, pulling a sexy cry of erotic pain from her lips.

Desperate to feel skin on skin, he rolled from the bed and quickly tore off his clothing, tossing it aside. Sophia, her eyes fixed on him, slipped off her panties and lifted her tunic over her head.

Returning to the bed, he lifted himself over her, he moved his right hand to her throat, circling it and pressing hard just beneath her jaw.

Her eyes widened as she stared up at him, her lips parting. "I'm going to claim you fully, Sophia Naomi Weinstein," he growled, power surging through his veins. "You will belong to me in every sense of the word."

"Yes," she whispered breathily, her pulse throbbing beneath his fingers around her throat.

All at once, she wriggled from his grasp and shifted so he fell away from her. She climbed over him, straddling his hips. Her nipples were erect, her dimples showing, her eyes sparkling, she said, "And you'll belong to me, too, Nicholas William Kincaid. Lock, stock and barrel."

Laughing, Nick flipped her easily over onto her back. Reaching for her arms, he circled her wrists and pressed them into the mattress over her head. "It's a deal," he said.

As he looked down at her, he lost himself in her gaze. "I am my beloved's," he whispered, the old biblical phrase for some reason leaping into his brain.

"And my beloved is mine," she replied softly.

Epilogue – Six Months Later

Sophia turned slowly, taking in the dimensions of the wonderful if rather rundown townhouse in London's Peckham district. It definitely needed work—lots of it—to bring it up to Impulse standards, but the bones of the place were good.

"What do you think?" Nick asked. "The price is high, but I think I could get it down a little. And even if I can't, it seems ideal for our first London club, don't you agree? It's got all those wonderful nooks and crannies where we could create little mini-dungeons for private play, and this downstairs space is perfect for the main gathering place."

"I love it," Sophia agreed. "We could set up the top floor with the VIP bedrooms, like you have back in New York. We could even add a small kitchen up there and put in a decent bathroom, so we could stay here while we're in town."

"Great idea," Nick said, taking her hand and giving it a squeeze. "I'm going to make a bid for it this afternoon. I've got a meeting with my broker, or estate agent, as they call them over here."

"Cool. And while you're doing that, there's this great vintage flea market I want to check out over on Church Street."

The last six months had been, hands down, the best of Sophia's life. Nick had been serious about selling his real estate business. And while his clubs and her shop still kept them each plenty busy, they came home at night to each other and made sure to take at least one day a week totally off.

Sophia had been surprised but pleased when Nick hadn't seemed to mind that she didn't want to move to his penthouse in Manhattan. He understood and accepted that she wanted to be closer to her shop, and to her family. Obviously, her studio apartment wouldn't do for both of them, but Nick had found a wonderful old, rambling single family home in Park Slope. They'd moved in together, and Sophia was having a great time fixing it up.

She, too, had made some compromises, giving Laura more authority and time at the shop, along with a much-deserved raise. She still went home to her parents for Friday night dinner at least once a month, and Nick was a welcome guest there. It had become something of a running joke between her mother and grandmother about the lovely babies the two of them would soon produce, once Nick made a proper woman of Sophia. They even forgave him for not being Jewish.

Nick laughed good-naturedly at their teasing, but Sophia was content to take her time. She did want children, and she wanted them with Nick, but they had lots of plans in the meantime. This visit to London was the first part of a two-month trip through Great Britain and the Continent. Sophia, who had never been outside the US, was having a blast.

She had to be careful though. During their travels, every time she so much as looked at a piece of art or a vase that might work for the shop or look good in their new home, Nick instantly bought it for her. Whether or not money was an object, Sophia still enjoyed hunting for the best deal. Her favorite finds were in tiny, cluttered stores filled with junk. Nick laughed indulgently at her unbounded joy when she unearthed potential gems among the rubbish.

One evening, Nick took her to an incredibly elegant restaurant in Mayfair. It was still hard for her to reconcile spending as much on a meal with wine as she would on a full month's rent of her old studio apartment, but Nick never batted an eye. When the main course had been cleared and they were enjoying raspberry cream gelato along with snifters of fine brandy, Nick pulled two small boxes from his jacket pocket and set them on the table.

Sophia's heart skipped several beats as she took in what was clearly a ring box, along with an oblong box that looked like it contained a necklace. Nick was often buying her bits of jewelry and trinkets she admired, but these looked serious.

He was smiling, though she could sense his nervous excitement. "Open this one first." He touched the necklace box.

Pulling it toward her, Sophia lifted the hinged lid. Inside was a rose gold pendant hanging from a delicate chain. At first glance, the delicate filigree etched onto it looked like a stylized heart. But upon closer inspection, she recognized the Impulse logo of a whip curved in the shape of a heart.

"It's beautiful," she said sincerely, running her finger over the delicate design.

"I know we aren't into the whole Master/slave thing. But I'd like you to wear this necklace as a token of your erotic submission to me, and my symbolic and loving dominance of you. Does that work for you, Sophia? Will you wear this necklace as a symbol of our unique BDSM connection?"

"Oh, yes, Nick. It would be my honor," Sophia breathed, happiness nearly lifting her out of her seat.

Nick held out his hand for the necklace, and she dropped it into his cupped palm. Getting to his feet, he moved around the table to her.

She lifted her hair and bent forward so he could place the chain around her neck. The pendant rested against her heart, as if it had always been there.

Nick returned to his seat, nodding with satisfaction as he gazed at her. "It's perfect," he pronounced. "Now, open the other box."

He bit his lip, the gesture sweetly vulnerable. She fell in love with him just a little more at that moment, if that was possible.

She opened the hinged lid of the box and drew in her breath. Nestled in the velvet were two rings of beaten gold, clearly antiques.

"Nick," she breathed. She lifted the smaller of the two rings from the box. It felt heavy and cool in her hands. "These are beautiful rings." She looked up at him, her heart in her throat.

"I found them in that antique jewelry store I

couldn't get you out of," he said with a laugh. "I didn't show you then because I wanted it to be a surprise. But clearly, they were made for us. Look at the inscription," he urged.

She tilted the ring to see the tiny calligraphic lettering inside: *I am my beloved's*, it read, echoing his sweet sentiment that fateful night when he'd come to her apartment. The quote was one from the Song of Songs, and was often used in marriage vows.

"Look at the second ring," he said.

She lifted the larger ring, clearly sized for a man, and peered at the inscription, which read: *My beloved is mine.*

"Is this…?" she asked stupidly. "Are you…?"

"Yes," he laughed. "It is. And I am. I want to spend the rest of my life with you. For now" — he took the smaller ring and reached for her right hand — "please wear this as a token of my love." He slipped the ring onto her finger. It fit perfectly.

"When we decide it's right for us, then I'll move that ring to your left hand."

Touched beyond words, Sophia reached for Nick's right hand. She slid the larger ring over his knuckle. The gold band suited him in its simple elegance.

"You know what this means, right?" she said, grinning at him. "The second my mother and grandmother get wind of this, they're going to be planning the wedding of the century. If you ever saw that movie, *My Big Fat Greek Wedding*, you'll know exactly what I'm talking about."

Nick laughed. "Don't worry. I'm sure we're up to whatever they throw our way. We'll let them do the whole big traditional thing, and then maybe we can have a private, more BDSM-themed ceremony of our own."

Sophia nodded eagerly. "That's a fabulous idea, Nick." She smiled goofily at him for a moment, and then she remembered.

"I have a surprise for you, too." Sophia reached into her bag for her phone. "I just got the confirmation."

She clicked on the screen to get what she wanted and then held it out to him.

It was an email from Desire Island confirming their spot on the waiting list, with an expected reservation date of nine months away. "I thought it would be fun to go back to where it all started," she said, feeling suddenly almost shy.

"Perfect," Nick enthused. "I love it." Then he

furrowed his brow and rubbed an imaginary beard. "I wonder if they do wedding ceremonies…"

Indie authors rely heavily on reviews to get the word out. Please take a moment to leave a quick review on Amazon.

And be sure to check out all the novellas in the *Desire Island Series* here:

https://www.amazon.com/gp/product/
B08298J19Y

Thanks, I really appreciate it! Claire